GENESIS GUNPLAY

Cody McCade rides into Genesis looking to uncover the truth about the sudden disappearance of the town's previous sheriff and the mystery of a young man's homestead, razed to the ground just before his wedding. But when up against local thugs and the deadly Shaw family, he realizes it will take more than asking around to get answers. However, the townsfolk have another mystery on their hands: just who is Cody McCade, and what brings him to Genesis?

JOHN DAVAGE

GENESIS GUNPLAY

Complete and Unabridged

LINFORD
Leicester

First published in Great Britain in 2013 by
Robert Hale Limited
London

First Linford Edition
published 2014
by arrangement with
Robert Hale Limited
London

A catalogue record for this book is available
from the British Library.

ISBN 978–1–4448–2209–0

Published by
F. A. Thorpe (Publishing)
Anstey, Leicestershire

Set by Words & Graphics Ltd.
Anstey, Leicestershire
Printed and bound in Great Britain by
T. J. International Ltd., Padstow, Cornwall

This book is printed on acid-free paper

Prologue

Driver Harry Watts cursed and pulled hard on the reins, bringing the Brynstone stage to a standstill yards from the three riders blocking the narrow box canyon. They were masked and armed with Winchesters.

Reacting fast, Ike Jones, Harry's shotgun rider, lifted his own rifle to respond, but three shots sounded simultaneously, echoing round the canyon, and Ike was shot dead before he could trigger it. Eyes staring into nothingness, he fell forward, bouncing off the rump of the nearest horse before hitting the ground with a thud.

Harry swallowed down bile and lifted his hands in the air in surrender. 'Don't shoot!' he yelled. 'I ain't armed!'

The trio of masked riders moved forward.

'Climb over the top and throw down

the bags,' the tallest of the three shouted to him.

Harry complied, his hands fumbling with the straps that held the baggage to the top and rear of the stage. As he began throwing the bags down, the stage door suddenly burst open and one of the three passengers jumped out, his .45 blazing.

None of his shots found a target.

'Bastards!' he shouted, before he was shot through the head and fell face down in the dirt.

Harry felt his innards turning to water.

'The other passengers!' the same masked rider yelled. 'Out! Hands in the air!'

There was a short pause, then first out was a short, tubby man with a grey goatee and wearing a striped suit and grey vest. He was mopping his face with a red handkerchief. Seconds later, he was followed by a slim, attractive woman dressed in a corduroy skirt and white shirt. On her head was a straw bonnet with a blue ribbon.

The two of them climbed meekly out into the hot sun, putting hands above their heads, their faces ashen with shock.

At the same time, Harry jumped down from the back of the stage, amongst the heap of luggage now scattered across the floor of the canyon.

All three stared at the masked men and waited.

Two of the three robbers were of a similar height and build, the third taller and slimmer. They were dressed almost identically in black. One of the two shorter riders pushed his Winchester into the scabbard at his side, took a canvas sack from inside his leather vest, then dismounted.

He walked across and frisked the driver, removing a handful of coins and dollar bills from Harry's pockets. Next he walked over to the passenger lying in the dust.

'Damn fool!' he grunted, turning the body over with his foot. The dead man was in his thirties, probably a cowhand. His pockets yielded just four dollars.

The masked man moved on to the man with the goatee. 'Empty your pockets, mister!' he growled.

The man began to bluster. 'This is outrageous! I — aagh!' He screamed as the back of the masked man's gloved hand smashed into his face.

'Do it! The watch, too!'

Whimpering, and trying to stem the flow of blood from his nose with his handkerchief, the older man pushed a wallet stuffed with dollar bills into the canvas sack. Then he pulled the timepiece from his vest pocket and dropped it in the sack with the money.

The masked man moved on to the woman. A gleam of lustful anticipation came into the grey eyes above the mask. But before he could put a hand on her, her own eyes narrowed and she spoke.

'I — I know you!' she said, suddenly. 'You're — !'

The shot rang out, echoing in the canyon, and a red patch spread slowly

4

beneath the woman's left breast. Her mouth opened in surprise, then her knees buckled and she slumped to the ground.

The speed with which the masked man had drawn his .45 left the stage driver open-mouthed with shock. 'You — you killed her! Why — ?'

'Shut up!' The masked bandit pressed the barrel of the .45 under Harry's chin. 'Empty the baggage an' put the valuables in the sack. An' do it fast!' He pushed the canvas sack into the driver's hand and shoved him towards the luggage.

Harry worked feverishly, from time to time glancing over his shoulder at the masked men. The bandit the woman appeared to have recognized was back on his horse, his Winchester resting across his lap.

It was in the dead woman's bag that Harry's hand encircled something small and hard. He recognized the shape. A small derringer, the kind a lady carried for protection! Harry's heart began to thump faster. His mouth was suddenly dry. Shielding it from the riders' view with his body and praying it was loaded, he removed the pistol and, still clutching it, eased it into the sack.

'Hurry!' the tallest of the riders shouted. 'What're you doin'?'

Harry turned, aimed the derringer at him, and fired. The bullet ripped through the top of the sack — but missed its target by a foot.

The tallest rider returned fire immediately, slugs thumping into Harry's chest before he fell down into the dust.

The tallest rider gigged his horse forward and retrieved the canvas sack, taking care to cover the hole made by the derringer so that its contents didn't spill out. Casually, he aimed his Winchester at the remaining passenger.

The man with the goatee felt a damp patch spreading at his groin. 'No!' he pleaded.

'Might as well be tidy, an' leave no witnesses,' the rider said — and fired.

Moments later, the three men removed

their masks and rode out of the canyon, leaving the five bodies sprawled in the dust. None of the riders checked to see that all five were dead.

A mistake.

If they had, they would have discovered that one was still breathing.

1

Cody McCade stared down at the blackened traces of the ranch house. A burn-out that was at least two or three weeks old, he reckoned. The ash was grey and all that was left of the building was the remains of the veranda steps leading up to a splintered, soot-streaked screen door, and the stone chimney in the centre of the rubble.

The sight sickened Cody. It reminded him of the hundred or more burn-outs he'd seen during the war — a war he'd spent the last twelve years trying to forget.

Still standing on the property were the corral fences and an arched gateway leading into what had until recently, Cody reckoned, been a medium-sized ranch. There was no sign of any animals. No sign of life anywhere.

Also victims of the inferno were the bunkhouse, the stable buildings and another smaller outhouse, probably the privy. All were some distance from the main house, too far for the flames to have spread accidentally. So this was no accidental fire. The place had been deliberately and systematically torched.

'Indians?' Cody muttered to himself, but almost as quickly dismissed the idea. He'd been travelling in this part of north Arizona for some weeks now, and hadn't set eyes on a single renegade in all that time.

He sat astride his stallion, a dun with a black face and tail, under the hot midday sun. He was a tall man, lean but muscular, with a shock of jet-black hair which had already begun greying at the sides despite his relatively young age of thirty-four. His features were sun-bronzed, but as hard and thin as a Bowie knife. He wore a black, flat-crowned hat, denim pants, a soft leather vest and a blue woollen shirt. A wide belt and holsters accommodated both his Peacemakers, and a scabbard at the side of his saddle held his Winchester.

Strapped behind him was a small carpetbag and saddle-bags.

Across the valley, an hour's ride away, was the huddle of mostly wooden buildings that made up the little town of Genesis — McCade's intended destination.

He patted his vest pocket and, satisfied that what was there could stay there until he was ready to reveal it, he said. 'Let's go,' and urged his stallion onwards.

2

Clete Jameson, sheriff of Genesis, stared bleakly at what he knew was a losing hand of cards and cursed. Sweat prickled his brow. Hands shaking, he took another slug of redeye from the shot glass in front of him before throwing the playing cards down onto the table and scowling across at the man opposite him.

Seth Shaw smiled, his mouth a crooked slash. 'You quit, Clete?' he said, scooping the loose coins from the table into his Stetson. He was in his mid-twenties, had a shock of rust-coloured hair and eyes the colour of cold ash.

'Yeah, I guess I do,' Clete replied. His words were becoming slurred and he was finding it difficult to think straight. He mopped his face with his shirt-sleeve.

It was early afternoon and the saloon was quiet. Three men sat at the bar, drinking and making small talk; two more sat at a table, each with a saloon girl draped around their shoulders. A fat guy in a patterned waistcoat tinkled desultorily on a honky-tonk piano as he sucked on a cigar.

This was the scene that confronted Cody McCade as he pushed through the batwing doors of the Silver Buck saloon. Conscious of the heads turning in his direction, he took a careful look around the room. It took a moment to spot the face he had expected to see and he made his way across to the table.

'Howdy, Major,' he said.

The sheriff turned and stared at him, and Cody took in the bloodshot, unfocused eyes of a drunk. He also noted the slack jowls and thickening gut of a man badly out of shape. Clete was the same age as McCade but looked ten years older.

Clete stared at him for several

13

seconds before registering a sign of recognition.

'Captain McCade?' he said.

'Just plain Cody McCade, nowadays, Clete,' Cody replied. 'War's been over a long time.' He glanced across at the young man sitting opposite Jameson. 'Goin' to introduce me to your young friend?'

'Uh, sure,' Clete said. 'This is Seth Shaw. His pa, Judah Shaw, owns a big spread south of the town, an' . . . well, most of the businesses in Genesis.'

Cody nodded to Shaw, who was watching him with interest, then turned back to Clete. 'Your deputy told me I'd find you here,' he went on. 'Reckoned you spent most of your time in this place.'

Clete scowled. 'Ain't none of Chalky's business where I spend my time, jus' so long as I do my job.'

Seth Shaw stood up. 'Guess I'll be goin', Clete.' He looked at Cody. 'You plannin' to stay in Genesis a while, McCade?'

Cody shrugged. 'Kinda depends on things.'

'You an' Clete were in the army together?'

Cody nodded. 'Clete was my major for a time. Right, Clete?' There was a slight mocking note in his voice.

Clete avoided his gaze. He looked less than pleased to be reminded of this. 'Like you said, Captain, it was a long time ago. Things . . . change.'

Seth Shaw gave a short mocking laugh. 'They sure do! Gotta go, Clete. See ya around, McCade.'

The two men watched him leave, then Cody signalled to the barkeep that he wanted a beer and sat down in the chair Seth Shaw had vacated.

The two men were silent until Cody had his beer in front of him.

'How'd you hear I'd settled in Genesis?' Clete asked eventually. 'That I was sheriff here.'

'Got the word from a lawman, in Brynstone Creek,' Cody said. He sipped his beer. 'So tell me, how long

15

have you been here?'

Clete fingered the redeye bottle, clearly wanting to take a drink. After a moment, he poured a shot into the glass and gulped it down. ''Bout six years,' he said eventually. 'Drifted for some time after the war, then landed up here an' jus' stayed. Worked on Judah Shaw's spread for a time then he — that is, the town — made me sheriff three years ago.'

'Seem to remember you had a wife,' Cody said, watching him carefully. 'You have any family?'

'My first wife . . . died,' Clete said. 'We never had no kids. I — I married again. Della an' me been married eighteen months now.'

Cody took a long drink before placing the glass in front of him. 'You got married during the war,' he said after a moment.

Clete took a quick drink before answering, 'Yeah. Like I said, Rose.'

Cody waited expectantly for him to go on.

'What've you been doin' since the war, Captain?' Clete asked, clearly anxious to change the subject.

'Listen, Jameson, you can drop the 'captain',' Cody said. 'I guess you don't use 'major' any more, either.' He added, 'I've just moved around.'

'No wife?' Clete said.

'No,' Cody said, after a moment. His tone didn't encourage further questions and Jameson took the hint.

At that moment, a stocky, red-faced man moved away from the bar and passed by their table on his way to the batwings. 'Hey, Clete!' he rasped, grinning from under his walrus moustache. 'Tell Della, she ever wan' a real man to keep her warm a' nights, Joe Overton's available!'

Laughter came from the other men at the bar, together with a few bawdy comments.

Clete's face reddened and his hands shook as he gripped the shot glass between them. Cody McCade stared at him, waiting for a response. When none came, he stood up and put a hand on Overton's shoulder, forcing the other man to turn round.

'Just a second, mister,' he said. 'Seems to me you owe the sheriff an apology.'

'Who'n hell are you?' Overton snapped. Then something in Cody's cold gaze made him hesitate. 'I . . . that is . . .'

'Makes no never-mind who I am,' Cody said quietly. 'Just apologize to Jameson for insulting his wife.'

Overton glanced around the room, conscious that he was losing face but unsure what to do. 'I didn' mean nothin' by it. Just joshin' the sheriff, that's all,' he said.

'Apologize,' Cody said, his voice quiet but deadly. 'Or come outside.'

Overton swallowed. He looked at Clete, who still sat at the table staring at the shot glass, his hands shaking. Then he looked at Cody's .45s and made a decision. 'I — I'm sorry, Clete,' he muttered. 'No offence.' Then he turned and hurried from the saloon without looking back.

The tension in the room evaporated with Overton's departure, but the remaining men looked at Cody with a new respect.

Cody drank the last of his beer, then said, 'Let's go back to your office, Clete.'

3

Genesis's deserted main street baked under the iron-fist blaze of the afternoon sun. Two old-timers sat sleeping in chairs on the boardwalk outside the saloon. Nothing stirred.

Cody glanced up and down.

Across from the Silver Buck saloon was a general store, a barber shop, the bank, then a few houses with small yards in front of them, most of them neatly kept.

Down the street on the same side as the saloon was the hotel, and beyond that the livery and two or three more stores. The sheriff's office and jailhouse was a low adobe building. Hitching posts stood at intervals along the street.

At the southern end was a wooden church and schoolhouse. At the northern end was a mercantile and a feed store and, on the other side of an alleyway, the premises of the *Genesis Bugle*.

Cody had made a careful survey of all this on his way into town earlier. 'I'll meet you at your office in a few minutes, Clete,' he said now. 'I need to stable my horse.'

'Sure,' Clete said, avoiding Cody's eye.

Cody watched him move unsteadily along the boardwalk. Then he un-hitched his horse from in front of the saloon and walked the stallion the short distance to the livery.

Oakie Dawson took Cody's stallion and led it into a stall. 'Nice horse,' he said. 'How long you want me to stable him?'

'Can't say, for sure,' Cody said.

'Saw you come out of the Silver Buck with Clete Jameson, our excuse for a sheriff,' Oakie said. He was a short, stooped man with a lined face, an almost toothless mouth, and thinning grey hair. 'You a friend of his?'

'Knew him in the war,' Cody said.

'Tell me, who appointed Jameson sheriff?'

'Judah Shaw,' Oakie said. He spat on the straw. 'Shaw owns this town, mister, more's the pity. Made Clete sheriff after Phil Temple, the previous sheriff . . . well, he left kinda sudden.'

'Left for no reason?'

Oakie stared at Cody for several moments, then, seeming to make a decision, said, 'It was kinda mysterious. Shaw, who owns the bank, reckoned Phil stole $2,000 from the bank an' then took off.' He snorted. 'Bullshit! All we know is that Phil disappeared from Genesis one night an' nobody's seen him since.' He glanced around and lowered his voice. 'Some folks reckon Phil was gettin' to be a burr in Judah Shaw's pants 'cause he was askin' awkward questions about Shaw's two sons.'

'That right?' Cody said.

'So folks reckon,' Oakie said.

'So you reckon Shaw got rid of Temple?' Cody asked.

Oakie shrugged. 'Shaw an' his two sons — Zeke and Seth — don't give a damn what they have to do an' who they have to hurt to get what they want around here. They're both nigh-on plumb loco. If you're plannin' on stayin' in Genesis, mister, keep clear of the Shaws, that's my advice.'

Cody grimaced. 'That might be difficult,' he said.

4

Chalky Smith was sitting in the swivel chair behind Jameson's desk as the sheriff came in. The deputy immediately vacated it and moved to a chair in the corner of the room. Beside this, a door led to the two cells, and beyond that to the sheriff's quarters.

'You see your friend?' Chalky asked. He was a skinny, baby-faced eighteen-year-old with a lazy eye. He was attempting to grow a moustache, but it was little more than a dark shadow above his upper lip.

'Ain't no friend, 'specially. Just someone who served under me in the war. An' you can watch your mouth in future,' Clete told him. 'Sayin' I spend my days at the saloon.'

Chalky yawned. 'No more'n the truth,' he replied.

Clete strode across and cuffed the

youngster across the ear. 'Get out an' patrol the street. Make like you're doin' your job for once!'

Chalky swore softly and stumbled across to the door, rubbing his ear. As he went out into the street, he passed Cody McCade on the boardwalk. 'Sheriff's inside,' he muttered, sullenly.

'Fresh kid,' Clete said when Cody entered, carrying his saddle-bags and carpetbag. 'Don't know why I put up with him.'

'He the only help you've got?' Cody asked. He perched on the edge of Clete's desk, dropping his saddle-bags and carpetbag on the floor.

Clete nodded. 'Don't really need him. Town's pretty law-abidin' most of the time.'

'That right?' Cody said. 'Only I passed a burnt-out ranch in the valley, coupla miles north of town. Didn't look like an accidental fire to me. Reckon it was torched.'

Clete looked at his hands. 'Yeah, that would be Ben Paton's place. Renegade

Indians, we reckon. Took the horses an' burned out the buildings. Ben died in the fire.'

'Yeah?' Cody said. 'He have anybody working for him?'

'Two men. Ain't seen 'em since the fire. Indians prob'ly took 'em.'

Cody was silent for some moments, then he said, 'Clete, I haven't seen hide nor hair of a redskin in months. That wasn't the work of Indians, and you know it.'

Clete slammed the top of his desk with his fist. 'Listen, McCade! Just stay outa things an' you'll be welcome around here. Go stirrin' up trouble an' folks'll — '

He stopped suddenly as the door opened and a woman entered. She was tall and full-figured with shiny black hair that hung loosely around her shoulders. Her rouged face wore a sour expression as she came in, but quickly broke into an artificial smile when she saw Cody.

'Why, Clete, darlin', who have we

here?' she said, her voice low and throaty.

'Della, this is Captain — uh, Cody McCade,' Clete said. He glanced at McCade. 'This is Della, my — uh, wife.'

'Glad to meet you, Della,' Cody said, holding out his hand and trying to ignore the flirtatious look in her eyes.

She took his hand in hers, hanging on to it a moment longer than necessary. 'Nice to meet you, Captain.'

'Just Cody.' He recognized the smell of brandy on her breath and recalled that he hadn't seen her in the saloon. So where — and with whom — had she been drinking? 'I've dropped the 'captain',' he told her. 'Clete, is there a rooming house in town? Reckon the hotel prices'll be a mite too fancy for my pocket.'

'Well ... ' Clete seemed to be reluctant to offer a suggestion.

'Come on, Clete,' Della said. 'There's only one roomin'-house in town, an' that's the Barrett place, down by the church.' She aimed her smile at Cody. 'You can't miss it. Got a fancy white picket fence around it. You'll prob'ly enjoy the company of Cathy Barrett, Mr McCade. She's kinda available now Ben Paton's not around anymore. 'Course, you'll have to watch out for Zeke Shaw. Reckon he's got plans for the prissy Miss Barrett.'

'Shut up, Della!' Clete barked.

Cody looked from one to the other in the silence that followed. 'Down by the church, you said. OK, guess I'll give it a try. Nice meetin' you, Mrs Jameson.' He picked up his bags and went out of the door.

Almost immediately, Clete got up from his chair and grabbed his wife by the arm. 'Where'n hell you been?' he barked. 'I can smell the booze on your breath from across the room! An' who've you been with?'

'Mind your own damn business!' she snapped, yanking her arm from his grasp. And she stormed through to the back rooms.

Clete watched her, a bleak look of despair in his eyes, then he sank back down in his chair and pulled a fresh bottle of redeye from his desk drawer. His hands shook as he uncorked it and held it to his lips.

5

Cody approached the white picket fence surrounding the yard of the rooming house and opened the gate. He gave a friendly slap to the rump of the sorrel that was tethered to the gatepost and walked up the path.

The door of the house was ajar and Cody heard a woman's voice as he was about to knock.

'Zeke, I can't — it's not — it's too soon,' she was saying. 'Now, please go.'

'Listen, Cathy,' a man's voice replied. 'Ben Paton's dead, there ain't no changin' that.'

'Please, Zeke, just leave. Pa will be finishing his nap, and — '

'I ain't leavin' till you answer me. You know how I feel about you, an' — '

It was at that moment that Cody decided to make his presence known.

'Excuse me, ma'am?' he said, knocking and gently pushing the door inwards to reveal the two figures inside. 'I'm looking for a room.'

The girl was nineteen or twenty years old — tall and slim with red-gold hair and fine-boned features. She wore a shirtwaister dress. Cody thought her very beautiful. The man was older, well built with rust-coloured hair, and his resemblance to Seth Shaw was noticeable, though he was probably a year or so younger. Like his brother, he had a snake-like wariness about him, and he did not look pleased by Cody's interruption.

He glanced in Cody's direction, scowled, then turned his back on him. 'Get lost, mister,' he said over his shoulder. 'Me an' the lady are talkin'.'

'I reckon I heard the lady ask you to leave,' Cody said, quietly. 'Maybe you should do just that.'

Zeke Shaw spun on his heel. 'I tol' you to get lost!' he yelled.

'Zeke, please,' Cathy Barrett began.

She was suddenly afraid for the newcomer. 'There's no need to . . . '

Her voice trailed off as Cody stepped into the hallway and opened the door wide behind him, an obvious invitation for Zeke Shaw to leave. He dropped his carpetbag and saddle-bags on the floor beside him. His eyes never left those of the young man and a slow smile spread across his face. 'Goodbye, Mister Shaw,' he said.

'Goodbye, hell!' Zeke retorted, and went for the six-shooter that was tucked into his belt — only to feel the iron grip of Cody's hand round his wrist and the .45 whipped from his grasp.

Zeke took a swing with his free hand, but the punch didn't connect. Cody dodged it and put the young man's arm into a hammerlock before turning him round and putting a boot into the small of his back. He shoved him out of the door so that Zeke fell sprawling face-down onto the path, sucking up a mouthful of dust.

Cody stuffed Zeke's gun into his belt.

'I'll give your six-shooter to your pa,' he told the youngster. 'Seems likely I'll be seeing him sometime.'

'You sure will, mister!' Zeke shouted, getting to his feet and spitting dust from his mouth. 'An' if'n he don't kill you, I sure as hell will, you can rely on that!' He stumbled out of the gate towards his horse, not looking back.

Cathy waited until he was astride the sorrel and riding away before speaking. Then she looked at Cody and said, 'I don't know who you are, but you've just made yourself a powerful enemy. The Shaws — '

'I've heard about the Shaws,' Cody interrupted, smiling. 'But I'm still looking for a room and I hear this is a rooming house.'

'It is,' Cathy admitted. 'And — well — we do have a room available. Even so, after your, er, exchange with Zeke Shaw, I recommend you make your stay in Genesis a short one.'

Cody picked up his bags. 'I'll bear that in mind, ma'am.'

'It's miss, but please call me Cathy,' she said.

'Name's Cody McCade,' he told her, shaking the delicate hand that she offered. 'Glad to make your acquaintance.'

'I'll show you the room, Mr McCade,' she said. 'Supper's at six, if you'd care to join us. There's just me, my pa and our one other boarder — Jim Cranston, the editor of the *Genesis Bugle*.'

'I'll look forward to that, Cathy,' he said. 'Meantime, I think I'll take a siesta. I've had a hard few days ridin'.'

6

Judah Shaw was fifty years old, stood six foot six inches tall and weighed two hundred and fifty pounds. A big man in every sense of the word. His thick shock of hair had turned snowy-white ten years ago, on the death of his first wife, Emma. She had been kidnapped and killed by Comanche Indians whilst he was away buying horses for the Triple S ranch.

Her death had 'turned' Judah. He had quickly become a bitter, ruthless and unscrupulous man who cared little about anything other than the acquisition of land and property. Within two years of Emma's death, he had quadrupled the amount of land he possessed, started up the Genesis bank and the *Bugle* newspaper, and held mortgages on two-thirds of the local businesses.

That his methods of procurement didn't bear honest scrutiny mattered little to Judah Shaw. What he wanted, he took. And he'd brought his two sons up the same way.

Then, just over two years ago, he had met Mamie Harper on a rare trip east, and had been bewitched by her charm and gentle beauty. Mamie came from a good family, and when she eventually succumbed to Judah's persuasive overtures, she came west against the wishes and pleadings of both her parents and her two sisters.

At this moment she was resting in the cool of her bedroom whilst Judah was listening to Seth's account of his meeting with McCade. The two men were in the spacious living room of the Triple S ranch house. Judah was sitting in a huge leather armchair, puffing on a cheroot. Seth was perched on the arm of the chair opposite him.

'He knew Jameson in the war,' Seth was saying. 'Not sure how long he's plannin' to stay in town.'

'Look like trouble?' Judah asked.

Seth shrugged. 'Hard to say, Pa. Although I met a coupla guys from the saloon after I'd picked up the things we needed from the mercantile. They reckoned McCade faced up to Joe Overton after Overton made some remark about Della to Clete. McCade made Joe look a damn fool.'

'That's not difficult,' Judah said. 'Overton's got a big mouth. It'll get him killed, one of these days.'

Both men looked up as Zeke stormed into the room, his face contorted with rage.

'So who put a burr in your britches?' Seth asked, grinning at his younger brother.

'Some ornery critter who busted in while I was talkin' to Cathy,' Zeke growled.

'What'd he look like?' Seth wanted to know, suddenly suspicious.

''Bout six foot, black hair, packs a coupl'a .45s in tied-down holsters.'

Seth and his father exchanged looks,

then Seth glanced at Zeke's belt. 'What happened to your six-shooter?'

'Bastard took it, didn't he!' Zeke said. 'I'm gonna kill him next time I see him!'

'Good idea,' Seth said. 'If — '

'Listen! Neither of you are going to do anything until I learn a bit more about this man McCade,' Judah said quietly but firmly.

Zeke stared at his father. 'McCade? Is that his name? You know him, Pa?'

'Seth's been telling me about him,' Judah said.

'He's a friend of Clete Jameson,' Seth explained to his brother.

'Is he, dammit!' Zeke said.

'Yeah,' Seth said. 'What'd you do to rile him, brother?'

'Nothin'! I was talkin' to Cathy an — '

'Pesterin' her, more like,' Seth said. 'Askin' her to marry you, yet again.'

'What if I was?'

'Ain't you got the message, Zeke? She ain't interested.'

'She will be!' Zeke snapped.

Judah checked the time on the longcase clock in the corner of the room. 'I'm going into town to the bank for a spell,' he announced. He looked at Zeke. 'Keep your temper under control until I learn more about this man, McCade. Do you understand?'

Zeke looked away. 'Sure, Pa,' he said.

7

Jim Cranston was drinking coffee in Porky Tyler's café. It being a particularly quiet time of the late afternoon, Porky had come to sit with him, nursing his own mug of coffee.

Cranston was twenty-five years old, slightly built and with a mop of fair hair. The young editor, reporter and printer of the *Genesis Bugle* was unloading his troubles on the sympathetic ear of the café owner.

Porky was twice Jim's age and shaped like a beer keg under his food-stained apron. He sported bushy side whiskers that almost met under his chin and a pair of wire-rimmed eyeglasses through which he peered myopically.

'You're in a bad way, young'un,' he said. 'Love — a love that ain't returned — can be the undoin' of a man. Makes 'em prone to do stupid things.' He looked at Jim with a serious expression. 'Like facin' up to Zeke Shaw. If'n he gets the idea you're sweet on Cathy Barrett, he's as likely to kill you as look at you.'

'I know,' Jim said.

'An' you ain't as fast with a gun as the characters you write about in those dime novels you pen in your spare time,' Porky reminded him.

'I know that too,' Jim admitted. 'But I can't just stand by and let her marry that rattlesnake!'

'Think that's likely? I know the Shaws can be powerful persuasive, but Cathy's got a sensible head on her shoulders.'

'Her pa's a sick man. He can't have more than a few more months to live, according to Doc Hamlin. That rooming house is mortgaged to Judah Shaw's bank and there's a loan.'

'So what're you sayin'?' Porky said. 'That Judah Shaw'll bring financial pressure to bear on ole man Barrett, if'n he decides Zeke needs a little help

41

makin' Cathy say yes?'

'I'm not saying he would, I'm just saying he could,' Jim said.

Porky sipped his coffee then looked across the top of his mug at his young friend. 'How does Cathy feel about you, has she said?'

Jim shook his head. 'It's as if she's afraid to say anything, but I can see in her eyes she's got feelings for me.' He sniffed. 'Not that I've got much to offer her. What am I? Editor of Judah Shaw's newspaper — in other words, his mouthpiece whenever he wants the townsfolk to know something. He pays my wages, I write what I'm told. Jeeze, Porky, I'm as bad as Clete Jameson! Just another Shaw stooge!'

Porky put a hand on Jim's arm. 'Don't be too hard on yourself, kid. Judah Shaw owns pretty much everybody in this town. Guess it's only a matter of time before he decides to find a way to buy me out, too. Like most folk, I owe money to his damn bank.'

The two men stared moodily into their mugs, in silent agreement about the unfairness of life in Genesis but uncertain what to do about it.

8

Judah Shaw closed his office door in the bank just after five that evening. He looked across at the grey-haired figure stooped over the counter.

'Can you finish things up, Henry?' he said to his chief clerk.

Henry Rees nodded. 'Certainly, Mr Shaw,' he said.

Judah was about to head back to the Triple S when a thought occurred to him and he changed his mind. Instead, he went outside and directed his mount towards the Bassett rooming house.

Minutes later, he was knocking the front door and removing his Stetson.

Cathy was both surprised and alarmed to see Zeke Shaw's father standing outside when she opened the door.

'Wh-why, Mr Shaw,' she said, looking up at him. He towered over her in the doorway. 'This is a surprise.'

He smiled. 'I gather you have a new boarder, Cathy,' he said. 'May I speak with him, if he's in?'

'Uh — yes, of course,' she said, stepping back to allow him inside. 'Go through to the parlour. Pa's there. I'll — I'll just fetch Mr McCade.'

She disappeared up the stairs as Judah walked through to the front room of the house.

A frail figure sat in a wheelchair in one corner, his legs wrapped in a blanket in spite of the heat coming from a fire in the hearth.

'Thought I heard your voice, Shaw,' Owen Barrett said. He looked like a man of seventy instead of forty-five. The cancer that was eating away at his insides had reduced him to a near-translucent skeleton.

'How are you, Owen?' Judah asked.

'Dying, as you well know, Shaw,' Owen replied. 'Doc Hamlin doubts I'll see Christmas. Oh, he doesn't say as much, but I can see it in his eyes every time he looks at me.'

'Cathy aware of that?'

'Sure, but we don't talk about it.' He frowned. 'So you came to see our new boarder?'

Judah nodded. 'That's right. I believe he's got something that belongs to Zeke.'

'I haven't met him yet myself,' Owen said. 'I was resting when he arrived, and he was taking a siesta when I got up.'

Judah was about to say something else when they heard Cathy and McCade coming down the stairs. A moment later, the two of them came into the parlour. McCade had a .45 tucked into his belt.

Cathy made the introductions.

'Glad to meet you, Mr McCade,' her father said. A gleam came into his eye. 'I hear you had a bit of a set-to with young Zeke earlier.'

'I heard that, too, McCade,' Judah said smoothly. He smiled. 'Allow me to apologize for my son. He can be a little hot-tempered sometimes.' He looked at

Cathy. 'Especially when it involves his sweetheart.'

Her face reddened but she said nothing.

'Zeke, like his pa, presumes too much!' Owen Barrett said, an edge to his voice and his face darkening.

Judah Shaw just shrugged and smiled again.

Cody removed the .45 from his belt and held it out to Judah.

'Give this back to your son, Shaw,' he said, his face an unreadable mask. 'But tell him if he ever tries to draw it on me again, it'll be the last thing he does.'

The smile on Judah's face slipped. After a moment, he took the gun.

'I'll mention that to Zeke,' he said quietly. He stared at Cody for several seconds, as if sizing him up, then glanced at Cathy and her father. 'Now, if you'll excuse me, I have to be getting back to the ranch.' He tucked the .45 under his black coat and looked steadily at McCade. 'It's been very . . . interesting meeting you, McCade.'

'No doubt we'll meet again,' Cody said.

Judah gave a humourless smile. 'Oh, you can count on that,' he said.

9

The three men sat round the long pine kitchen table, Owen in his wheelchair. Supper over, Cathy was pouring coffee for each of them from a flowered jug. Owen had eaten hardly anything, but McCade and Jim had tucked into a tasty stew.

Jim had spent most of the meal trying to extract information from and about Cody at the same time as following Cathy's every movement. He'd been largely unsuccessful with the former.

'You ever married, Cody?' he asked.

Cody took a long draught of coffee before replying. 'Nope.'

'Jim writes dime novels, Mr McCade,' Owen explained. 'He's got one of those new-fangled typewriting machines in his room. No doubt you'll hear him working it, seeing as your room is next to his.'

'That a fact,' Cody said.

'Sends them to a company in New York,' Owen went on. 'Had a couple printed, too. That right, Jim?'

The young writer nodded. 'Yes.'

'He bases his story heroes on real people,' Owen said. He gave a wheezy chuckle. 'So now you know why he's been pumping you with questions all through supper, Mr McCade. He's hoping you've done something worth writing about.'

'Pa, stop it. You're embarrassing both of them,' Cathy said.

'Sorry to disappoint you,' Cody said to Jim. 'I'm no hero.'

Jim gave him a smile. 'Judging by the way you handled Zeke Shaw and his father, I'd say the jury's out on that.'

The three men drank their coffee in an awkward silence for some minutes. Cathy poured herself a cup and sat down.

After a time, Cody turned towards her. 'If it's not too painful a subject, Cathy,' he said, 'can you tell me more about what happened to Ben Paton? I've gathered you and he had an — er — understanding.'

'We were going to be married,' Cathy said, her voice trembling. 'He — he died in the fire at his ranch. Sheriff Jameson thinks it was attacked by Indians.'

'Which is ridiculous,' Owen Barrett said. 'We all know there hasn't been an Indian in this territory for at least two years, never mind a renegade bunch.'

'So, if it wasn't Indians, who . . . ?' Cody began.

'Zeke Shaw,' Jim said. 'Or on his orders.'

'Why?' asked Cody. 'Do the Shaws want Paton's land?'

'Maybe,' Owen said.

He and Jim exchanged glances but seemed reluctant to go on.

'Something you're not telling me?' Cody asked.

Cathy Barrett sighed. 'They think Zeke murdered Ben so that he could have me!' she said. 'There, now I've said it!' She looked at Jim and her father. 'You two have been pussy-footing around the subject for weeks now, afraid of upsetting me, but I've known all along what you were thinking.'

'Do you believe it, Cathy?' Cody asked.

There were tears in her eyes as she struggled to control her emotions. 'I just don't know. I can't believe even Zeke Shaw would do such a thing, but . . .'

'Ben was also one of the few people in Genesis who didn't have a mortgage with Shaw's bank, so Judah had no hold on him that way,' Owen said. 'Couldn't force him off his land for defaulting on mortgage payments, the way he's stolen — yes, I use the word advisedly — stolen other folks' property.'

'Also, Ben was critical of Judah Shaw's methods,' Cathy said. 'He was getting a group of townsfolk together, including Doc Hamlin, to oppose Shaw at the mayoral elections last month. Ben was even talking of standing for mayor himself.'

'He wrote several anti-Shaw letters to

the *Bugle*,' Jim said. 'I got into a whole heap of trouble with Judah Shaw for printing them, but for once I didn't care.'

'Shaw doesn't like anybody disagreeing with him,' Owen said.

'It was soon after that somebody burned Ben's ranch house,' Jim went on. 'His two ranch hands, Jake Finney and Len Walker, were in town that evening. They arrived back at the ranch to find it ablaze. There was nothing they could do. Lost most of their own things too. We reckon that both men, guessing who was behind the fire and not wanting to cross Shaw, decided to take off the next day. They've not come back.'

'And the sheriff?' Cody queried.

'Clete Jameson did nothing. Just swallowed the tale Shaw spread about Indians torching the place,' Owen said, his face even greyer with fatigue now. 'I don't wish to speak ill of your old army friend, Mr McCade, but Clete was a poor replacement for our last sheriff, Phil Temple. You heard what happened to him?'

'I heard the story,' Cody said. 'It seems he stole $2,000 from the bank and took off with it.'

'You're right when you say it's the story,' Jim said. 'Not many folk believe it.'

'Even so, he hasn't come back,' Cody said.

'No,' Jim admitted. 'One way or another, the Shaws have seen to that.'

'It's a damn shame,' Owen said. 'Phil Temple was a fine man. I don't believe for one moment that he stole any money.'

'Nor do most folk,' Cathy said.

Owen drained the last of his coffee then, with an effort, eased his wheel-chair away from the table.

'You all right, Pa?' Cathy said.

'I'm fine, but I guess I'll turn in, Cathy,' Owen said. 'I'm feeling a little tired suddenly.' He nodded towards Cody. 'Good to have you with us, Mr McCade.'

He wheeled his chair through the kitchen doorway to his bedroom at the back of the house. Cathy went after him to see that he had all he needed for the night.

'Guess you've noticed he's dying,' Jim said softly, when both were out of earshot.

Cody nodded. 'I've noticed. It'll be tough on Cathy, when it happens. She'll need somebody strong to depend on.' He looked pointedly at the young man.

Jim's face reddened. 'I know.'

'Think I'll stretch my legs and get some air,' Cody said after a moment. 'Check on my horse and maybe get a drink at the saloon later. Coming with me, Jim?'

The young man glanced at the doorway through which Cathy had followed her father. 'Er — no, guess I'll stay here. Maybe go up and do a bit of writing later.'

Cody smiled to himself as he went out of the room.

10

Miss Lorelei's whorehouse adjoined the saloon, which was convenient for her clientele, many of whom made a beeline from one building to the other, buoyed up with redeye and Dutch courage, and hoping to be the man who could boast bedding Miss Lorelei herself. It was a lost cause. Lorelei kept her charms discreetly and exclusively for Judah Shaw.

She was in her mid-thirties and had the world-weary look of a woman who had seen it all. She had a fine full figure, and plum-coloured hair, which most of the time was piled high on her head but which looked mighty pretty when spread out on her silk pillow, as Judah had told her on many an occasion.

Each night, she sat in her little parlour, playing solitaire and sipping from a tumbler of brandy, her door open into the passage so that she could see who came and went. Tonight was no different from any other.

Upstairs, Seth Shaw was enjoying the delights of Sadie, one of Miss Lorelei's girls. In fact, he was enjoying himself rather too boisterously, to the point where Sadie began letting out ear-splitting screams.

Lorelei, who was protective of all her girls, lost no time in dropping her playing cards, picking up a wooden club which she kept by her side, and mounting the stairs in haste.

She barged into Sadie's room where she found Sadie pinioned to the brass bed with Seth on top of her, his hands round her throat, the pair of them buck naked. A purple bruise was beginning to swell up around Sadie's right eye.

'Oh, hell,' Lorelei muttered.

Moving swiftly, she used the club to whack Seth across his bare buttocks so that he let out a yell of pain before rolling off Sadie and onto the floor with a thump.

'What the — ?' he began.

'Get dressed an' get out!' Lorelei told him, scooping up his clothes and tossing them to him. She glanced at Sadie and saw bloody scratches on her breasts and thighs. 'An' don't come back, you animal!'

Seth looked murderous. He scrambled to his feet, rubbing his backside. Then, eyes blazing, he pulled on his pants and shirt. 'Cow!' he screamed at Lorelei. 'Bitch!'

As she watched him stumbling down the stairs, struggling to put on his boots whilst holding on to his gunbelt at the same time, not for the first time she told herself Seth Shaw was plumb loco and she'd been crazy to let him near one of her girls. Well, never again.

'You ain't heard the last of this!' he shouted from the street doorway, his features contorted with rage. 'If I tell my pa, he'll — '

'If I tell your pa what you did to

Sadie,' Lorelei retorted, 'he'll more'n likely whip you himself!'

Seth, his face a mask of humiliation, cursed and stormed out into the street where he saw Zeke going into the saloon next door. He took a half-step towards him, but changed his mind. Instead, not wanting to explain his half-dressed state to Zeke, he waited until his brother was out of sight before unhitching his horse and riding out of town.

The Silver Buck was bustling with activity; a line of men at the bar, others at tables playing poker or faro, and the pianist thumping out an indecipherable tune on the honky-tonk as he chewed on a cigar. Saloon girls weaved between the tables, shrieking, bumming drinks and avoiding wandering hands. A cacophony of noise filled the room, which was over-hung by a fog of tobacco smoke.

Zeke took in the scene then walked across to the bar. He slapped down a fist. The barkeep, moving quickly, placed a bottle of whiskey and a glass in front of him.

'Bad day, Zeke?' one of the men at the bar said, winking at and nudging his companion. 'Hear you lost your six-shooter. Kinda careless, that.' A grin started to spread across his face — but never made it all the way.

The back of Zeke's hand pounded the man's cheeks with such venomous force, it loosened three of the other's front teeth and produced a stream of blood from his nose.

'Yeah, I lost it, Reed!' Zeke snarled. He pushed the other man back against the bar, holding him round the throat with one hand and snatching Reed's six-shooter from its single holster with the other. 'That's why I'm takin' yours.' He placed the barrel under Reed's chin. 'OK?'

'Sure, Zeke,' Reed said, his voice little more than a croak. 'Sure, that's OK.'

After a tense twenty seconds, during which Reed stared into the crazed eyes and said a silent prayer, Zeke released him and stuffed the weapon into the waistband of his pants.

'Get lost,' he told Reed.

Reed wiped the blood from his face with the back of his hand, swallowed the last of his drink and made a swift beeline for the saloon batwings without looking back.

Zeke took a drink from the bottle of whiskey, ignoring the glass. The comforting feel of the six-shooter improved his mood somewhat. He looked around the room and, after a moment, saw the foreman of the Triple S sitting at a table near the batwings.

Charlie Newton had a buxom, red-haired saloon girl sprawled across his lap and he was pouring liquor into the shot glass she was holding in front of her.

Zeke watched the two of them enjoying a bout of horseplay for several minutes, then came to a decision. A decision that went in the face of his pa's instructions but for once Zeke didn't care. He picked up his bottle and walked across to the table.

'Howdy, Charlie,' he said, and carefully placed a bottle on the table. He glared at the girl. 'Get!' he told her.

For a moment she looked ready to protest, but then caught the cold gleam in Zeke's eye and retreated.

'Sorry to spoil your fun, Charlie,' Zeke said, sitting down at the table.

Newton shrugged, said nothing.

Zeke looked round, then lowered his voice. 'Got a job for you.'

'Yeah?' Newton said.

His eyes were devoid of any expression. Ten years older than Zeke, he was not afraid of the young hellion. But he was quick to recognize the kid's unstable — and therefore dangerous — state of mind. Besides, having heard what had happened to Zeke at the Barrett rooming house earlier that day, he already had an inkling of what was coming.

'Yeah,' Zeke said. He knew he was choosing his man wisely. Newton was a loner, rarely mixing or drinking with the other hands, and keeping his thoughts and opinions to himself.

He had also been the one who had shot and killed Ben Paton before he, with Zeke, had torched Paton's ranch. For this, Newton had been paid a substantial bonus in addition to his foreman's wages.

Newton unhurriedly built himself a smoke, then said, 'Let me guess. You want me to kill someone, an' you want me to do it when you ain't anywhere around. Right?'

Zeke nodded, a manic grin on his face.

'An' the fella you want dead,' Newton continued, 'is the same *hombre* who took away your six-shooter. Right?'

Zeke nodded.

'How much?' Newton asked.

'Same as for Paton,' Zeke told him. 'Fifty bucks.'

Newton sucked on his cigarette, then said. 'Fifty now, another fifty when I've done the job.'

'That's kinda steep, Charlie,' Zeke said.

'Hundred bucks?' Newton said. 'No it ain't. This critter sounds dangerous.'

Zeke ran his tongue across his lips and smiled a mirthless smile. 'OK,' he said, removing a money clip from his pocket and peeling off some bills. 'But do it tomorrow.'

11

Mamie Shaw watched her husband as he returned from the town, assessing his mood. From careful observation, she came to the conclusion that he hadn't spent the time at Miss Lorelei's whorehouse after leaving the bank, as was often his custom.

Mamie, a small, petite woman in her mid-thirties, was under no illusions about her husband. Since leaving the comforts of her home back east she had slowly come to realize that her parents and sisters had been right. She had been a fool to marry Judah Shaw. The man was a bully who had no qualms about killing anyone who got in his way. And his two sons — her stepsons, she thought with disgust — were no better. Wild animals, the pair of them.

Judah entered and gave her a

perfunctory kiss on the cheek. 'Supper?' he queried.

'I've eaten,' she told him, coolly. 'I wasn't sure what time you would be home. I'll go and tell Rosita to prepare something.'

He nodded. 'Fine.'

Mamie hesitated, then said, 'Where have you been, Judah? Not to . . . that woman.'

He eyed her coldly, then said, 'I paid a call on Owen Barrett.'

'I see,' she said. 'Don't tell me, Zeke's been pestering that daughter of his again. Someone should tell him that's a lost cause.'

'I have, but that wasn't the reason for my visit,' Judah replied. 'They have a new boarder, a man called McCade. Zeke had a bit of a set-to with him earlier today, and McCade took his gun away from him.'

'Really?' Mamie hid a smile. For someone to go up against a Shaw in Genesis was as pleasing to Mamie as it was surprising. 'I can imagine your crazy son's reaction to that,' she said. 'You'll need to keep an eye on him, Judah, he's liable to do something stupid.'

'I went to apologize to Cathy,' her husband said, annoyed by the note of satisfaction in her voice but choosing to ignore it for the moment. 'And McCade returned the gun to me.'

Mamie raised her eyebrows. 'Is that right?' she said, smiling. 'He sounds very interesting, this Mr McCade.'

He gave her an icy look. 'He does, doesn't he? Guess I'll need to keep an eye on him, too. He could be trouble.'

Whilst Mamie was in the kitchen, giving instructions about her husband's supper, Judah eased himself into a chair and kicked off his boots. He was lighting a cheroot when she returned.

'Your supper will be ready in half an hour,' she said. She sat down in a chair opposite him, and something in her expression gave him warning of what came next. 'I want you to stop going to . . . that woman. It's humiliating for me, and I won't stand for it!'

Judah drew heavily on his cheroot, then exhaled. His face had coloured to a dangerous shade of purple. 'You'll stand for whatever I tell you to stand for,' he said, with repressed rage. 'And if by 'that woman' you're referring to Miss Lorelei, I'll pay her a visit whenever I choose. The warmth and enthusiasm of her . . . charms goes some way towards making up for the wintry welcome I get on the odd occasion I venture into your bed. You're a cold bitch, Mamie.'

She was out of her chair and across to him like a jack rabbit. But before she could attack his face with her nails, he gripped her wrists with such force she screamed with pain.

He stood up and thrust her away from him in one movement, so that she fell back into the chair she'd vacated. Some strands of her ebony-black hair became unpinned and fell across her forehead.

'You're a filthy bully, Judah,' she said,

breathing heavily and massaging her wrists. 'But you should remember I know things. Things the good people of Genesis would be interested to hear about their mayor. Like your crazy son's involvement in Ben Paton's death.'

He stared at her silently, towering over her chair. 'Don't threaten me, Mamie,' he said, his voice like a splinter of ice. 'Believe me, it's not wise. Now, I'll take my supper with Rosita in the kitchen. Make sure you're in your room and out of my sight when I return.'

She watched him walk out of the room, then muttered to herself, 'Enough is enough!'

For some weeks Mamie had been trying to form a plan of escape (for that's how she saw it) from the Triple S, and back to the refuge of her parents' home back east. Now it was no longer a matter of if she should go, but when.

It wasn't Genesis or the townsfolk she wanted to get away from. Some of them, like Doc Hamlin and the Bassett girl, were real nice people. It was Judah and his two crazy sons whom she now perceived as a threat to her safety.

The problem was, her departure would have to be done without Judah realizing that she had no intention of coming back. And that would be fiendishly difficult because he was no fool. He would quickly see through any plan to visit her folks and would either insist on coming with her or would refuse to let her go. He hated her, yes, but he didn't easily release the things — or people — he 'owned'. Sometimes she wished he'd have a heart attack and just die.

She needed a distraction. She needed someone or something that could occupy Judah and his sons long enough for her to slip away before they realized she had gone.

But who or what?

McCade.

The thought struck Mamie like a

miniature bolt of lightning. Already Judah seemed worried about the man's sudden arrival in Genesis. Could he turn out to be the diversion she needed?

12

Charlie Newton spent the night in town, sleeping in one of the rooms above the saloon instead of returning to the Triple S. He wanted to be up early, ready to take any opportunity to fulfil the task Zeke Shaw had set him and earn his hundred dollars.

He ate a breakfast of ham and eggs at Porky Tyler's café. Then, taking his time over his mug of coffee, he looked along the street. From his vantage point at the table by the window, he could see the Barrett rooming house where McCade was boarding.

Charlie was in no hurry. He could wait.

Porky was watching him from the kitchen doorway. He noted the direction of Charlie's gaze, and began to put two and two together. He'd heard about Zeke Shaw's showdown with the stranger in town — the man, McCade — and he knew Zeke would waste little time in exacting his revenge. He also knew Zeke would probably delegate the job to somebody else. Like the Triple S foreman, Charlie Newton.

Who at this precise moment was keeping a careful eye on the Barrett rooming house where McCade was staying.

Porky picked up the coffee pot and went across to the table by the window.

'More coffee, Mr Newton?' he asked.

Charlie looked up briefly, then returned his gaze to the street. 'Yeah,' he said, pushing his mug across.

'You not workin' at the ranch this mornin'?' Porky said, pouring the hot liquid and avoiding Charlie's eye.

'Nope.'

'Got other plans?' Porky asked.

Charlie looked at him suspiciously. 'Nosey son-of-a-bitch, ain't you, Porky? Got somethin' on your mind?'

'No,' Porky said quickly. 'Jus' makin' conversation.'

'Well, I ain't in a conversin' mood, so get!' Charlie told him.

Porky hurried back to his kitchen as Charlie resumed his surveillance. Once there, he pulled off his apron and made an exit through the back door. Using the town's back alleys, he hurried to the sheriff's office.

Clete Jameson sat behind his desk, perusing the *Genesis Bugle*. He dropped the newspaper as Porky came in.

'It's about your old army friend,' Porky said without preamble. 'Reckon he's in danger.'

Clete looked less than pleased to be bothered by Porky's ramblings, but he was prepared to give him a hearing. 'What're you talkin,' about, Porky?' he asked.

Porky explained his suspicions as briefly as he could. 'Reckon this McCade fella could be livin' on borrowed time,' he said.

Clete listened, a familiar pain forming in his gut as Porky told his tale. When the café owner had finished,

74

Clete said, 'Can't do nothin' about somethin' you might be imaginin'. Can't go accusin' folks without no evidence.'

'You could warn McCade. He's a friend of yours, ain't he?'

'Not 'specially,' Clete said. 'Never was. Just a captain to my major. Anyway, he's able to take care of himself.'

He picked up his newspaper again as a clear hint for Porky to leave.

Porky stared at him. 'Well, don't say I didn't warn you,' he said. Then, getting no reply, he shrugged and went out of the office.

After he'd gone, Clete dropped the newspaper on his desk, screwed it into a ball and cursed. He'd little doubt that Porky's suspicions were justified, but he had no intention of looking for any kind of trouble that might involve Judah Shaw and his two deranged sons.

'You're on your own, McCade,' he said to himself.

When Porky arrived back at the café,

he was alarmed to see an empty table and a half-empty coffee mug by the window but no sign of Charlie Newton.

'Charlie left?' he asked an old-timer who was sitting at another table.

'Took off like he had a hornet in his pants,' the old-timer said.

'When?' Porky asked.

''Bout five minutes ago. Somethin' he saw in the street seemed to shift him mighty quick.'

More like someone, Porky thought, and cursed Genesis's lily-livered sheriff for doing the only thing he seemed capable of these days — sitting on his butt!

Charlie Newton had seen Jim Cranston and McCade leave the rooming house together, and make their way along the street towards the newspaper office, chatting amiably. The sight had pleased Charlie because the narrow passageway at the side of the *Bugle* office would be a perfect place to conceal himself and await McCade's exit. McCade would have to pass by the mouth of the passage any time he headed back to the main part of the town, thus making an easy target for Charlie.

Now, using the maze of side streets and passages, Charlie was making his way there.

13

Cody watched with interest as Jim Cranston set up type on the flatbed printing machine.

'Nothing contentious in this week's edition of the *Bugle*,' Jim informed him. 'Nothing for Judah Shaw to come chasing me about.'

'You do everything around here?' Cody asked.

'Yep,' Jim said. 'Editor, reporter, advertising manager, printer.'

'How come Shaw picked you for the job when he started up the paper?'

'I was scratching a living doing odd jobs around the town,' Jim explained. 'Washer-up in Porky's café, swamper at the saloon — and I was sleeping in Oakie Dawson's stables. The only thing I owned, apart from the clothes on my back, was my typewriting machine. Ted Hanks at the mercantile used to give me paper for free. I owe a lot to Ted. Anyway, Shaw heard I could string words together better than most folks in town, so he offered me the job of editing the newspaper he was starting up.'

Cody nodded. 'And you couldn't afford to say no,' he said.

'Darn right, I couldn't,' Jim said. 'With what he was prepared to pay me I could get a proper bed to sleep in and some half-decent meals in my belly. And he was quite happy for me to carry on trying to write my novels in my own time.'

'Nice of him,' Cody said. 'But the job came at a price.'

Jim made a face and nodded. 'I quickly came to realize the *Bugle* was nothing more than a mouthpiece for Shaw's ambitions to become the town's next mayor. And I guess it worked, because that's what he is. Anyway, after he was elected, he made sure the paper continued to push his views about every blessed thing. On the odd occasion I wrote an opposing view in an editorial, or published a letter in which someone didn't agree with him, he threatened to fire me. Or worse.'

'Sounds to me like he's got you hog-tied,' Cody said.

'But maybe not for much longer,' Jim said. 'I'm making a few bucks from my books now. Who knows? Pretty soon I may be able to manage without the money from this job. It's a shame, though, because I'd relish the chance to be a proper newspaperman.'

'I'd like to read one of your dime novels sometime,' Cody said.

'They're not great literature,' Jim said. 'I'm no Dickens or Twain. Guess I'm just living out my fantasies on paper, writing about the sort of man I'd like to be.' He gave a short laugh. 'Killing the bad guys and rescuing beautiful ladies.'

He worked on the typesetting in silence for several minutes, then Cody said, 'What do you know about Clete Jameson's wife?'

Jim looked embarrassed. 'Della? What d'you want to know?'

'She doesn't seem the sort to marry somebody like Clete. What did she do before they got wed?'

Jim hesitated, then said, 'She worked for Miss Lorelei.'

'You mean she was a whore,' Cody said.

'That's about it,' Jim admitted. 'Reckon she used Clete as a stepping stone to something better. And now — well . . . '

'Go on,' Cody said. 'And now?'

'Now she'll take her pleasures wherever and with whomever she fancies, if you know what I mean.'

'I know what you mean,' Cody said. 'How come you know this?'

'Most folks in town either know or have guessed,' Jim said. 'Reckon even Clete knows.'

'Then he's a damn fool,' Cody said. 'He's sure changed since the war. What happened to him?'

'Drink, mostly,' Jim said. 'He started

drinking even before his first wife died.'

Cody hesitated. 'Tell me what you know about her.'

'Her name was Rose. Nice lady. Too nice for Clete, folks reckoned. They'd been married four or five years. Got married during the war.' He frowned. 'Clete didn't treat her especially well and she was on her way to Brynstone to see her folks when she was killed. People say she wasn't planning to come back, but I don't know if that's true.'

'Killed,' Cody said.

'Yes,' Jim said. 'Murdered in cold blood, to be accurate. The stage she was travelling in was held up and she was shot, along with the two other passengers, the driver and the shotgun rider. They were robbed of their money and valuables.

'The driver reckoned that, although all three were masked, Rose Jameson recognized the voice of one of them. She started to say so when the guy just up and shot her dead. After that, they killed the others.'

'But the driver survived,' Cody said.

'Yes. When the stage didn't arrive in Brynstone, the sheriff there telegraphed Phil Temple, and Phil formed a posse and went looking for it. Found the stage and the bodies in a box canyon fifteen miles north of town. Harry Watts, the driver, was still breathing — just. He survived long enough to tell his tale. Died soon after, though.'

'If Rose knew one of the robbers then he could've been from Genesis,' Cody said.

Jim nodded. 'That's what Sheriff Temple reckoned.'

'Could the driver describe them?'

'Two youngish, one maybe a little older than the other. Third man older still, and taller. Know what else the driver said?'

'What?'

'He said the two younger men could've been brothers. Had the same shape faces — long and narrow — and the same colour hair under their Stetsons. Ginger.'

The two men looked at one another. 'Like Zeke and Seth Shaw,' Cody said eventually. There was no surprise in his voice.

'Temple never said that outright, but I reckon that's what he was thinking,' Jim said. 'No proof though. The Shaw brothers were a couple of young hellions in those days. Still are, as I guess you've noticed.'

'Did Clete know about Temple's suspicions?' Cody asked.

'Not sure. Anyway, Judah Shaw would have convinced him otherwise. Believe me, Cody, Shaw can be powerful persuasive when he needs to be.'

'So everyone keeps telling me,' Cody said. He looked at the clock on the wall. 'Guess maybe I'll go and have a long talk with Clete in his office. Any luck, it'll be too early for him to have started drinking.'

Jim shook his head. 'It's never too early for Clete.'

'See you later,' Cody said.

14

Charlie Newton heard the door of the *Bugle* office open and close from his position in the passageway. As soon as McCade came into view, he stepped out of the shadow of the feed store's wall and levelled his .45.

Moving from the shadows was his undoing. The glint of sunlight on the barrel of the .45 caught Cody's eye and was enough warning for him to drop down onto one knee, draw his own Peacemaker and fire, a split second after the boom from Charlie's gun.

Charlie's bullet missed Cody by a whisker, whilst Cody's first bullet took Charlie in the chest, spinning him round. The second caught the would-be slayer in the back of the head.

Cody was holstering his gun when Jim Cranston came running from the newspaper office. At the same time, the owner of the feed store rushed out from his premises.

'Cody, are you all right?' Jim said, urgently. 'What happened?'

Cody indicated the body sprawled in the passageway. It was face-down until the feed store owner moved tentatively towards him and turned him over.

'Charlie Newton!' he exclaimed. He looked at Cody. 'Jeeze, mister, you've killed the foreman of the Triple S!'

'Only after he tried to kill me,' Cody said.

'Even so, Judah Shaw ain't gonna be too pleased.'

'Artie's right, Cody,' Jim said. 'Might take a bit of explaining.' He frowned. 'Why would Newton want to kill you?'

'He a friend of Zeke Shaw?' Cody asked.

A look of understanding passed across Jim's face. 'Not a friend, exactly, but he could certainly be in the pay of Zeke,' he said. 'You think this was Zeke's attempt at exacting revenge for taking his gun away from him yesterday?'

'You took Zeke Shaw's gun away from him?' The feed store owner looked astonished. 'Don't you know the kid's half-loco?'

Cody looked down at the prone body. 'I do now.' He frowned suddenly, staring at the front of Newton's waistcoat. 'What's this?' he said, bending down and removing a fistful of sawbucks from the waistcoat pocket of the dead man. He counted them. 'Fifty dollars,' he said. 'Now that's interesting.'

By this time a small crowd of townsfolk were gathering round the mouth of the passage. After a moment, Clete Jameson pushed his way through them, Chalky Smith following him.

'What'n hell's goin' on here?' Clete wanted to know. His hands shook and he was already slurring his words. Then he saw the face of the victim and his own face purpled with a mixture of anger and embarrassment. 'Care to explain this, McCade?' he said, his voice shaking.

'He was waiting for me when I came out of the newspaper office, Clete,' Cody said calmly. 'The sun caught the barrel of his .45 as he took aim. Gave me just long enough to drop and for him to miss me.'

'An' you shot him,' Clete said.

'I did,' Cody said.

Clete shook his head, as if to clear it. 'Any witnesses?' he asked.

Cody stared at him silently. Then he said. 'No, Clete. Guess you're going to have to take my word for what happened. You got a problem with that?'

Clete sighed. 'Go fetch Jed Collins, the undertaker,' he told his deputy. 'McCade, you'd best come back to my office with me. Reckon I'd better take a statement. Judah Shaw's gonna want to know 'xactly what happened to his foreman when I ride out to the Triple S an' tell him. Jeeze, what a mess!'

'Sure thing, Clete,' Cody said. 'Oh,

and you'd better have these. They were in Newton's waistcoat pocket. Seems the Triple S are pretty generous with their foreman's pay.' He handed over the dollar bills.

Clete stared at the money, then looked at Jim Cranston. 'That right? These were in Charlie's pocket?'

Jim nodded. 'They were,' he said. 'Reckon he was in the pay of someone, don't you, Clete? Now, I wonder who?'

The sheriff's face paled as he pushed the money into his own vest pocket, then said, 'C'mon, McCade.'

The townsfolk parted to let the two men through. Porky Tyler was one of the crowd and glared angrily at Clete. He was about to say something, until he caught the sheriff's warning glance and changed his mind.

15

Zeke Shaw paced the floor of his room in the Triple S ranch house. Every few minutes he looked out of the window to see if Charlie Newton was returning from Genesis with the news he was waiting for — that the man calling himself McCade was dead. Damn it, it was nearly midday! Surely the deed would have been done by now.

Across the yard in the corral, he could see his father and brother examining a new mare with one of the ranch hands. Suddenly, all three men turned and looked in the same direction.

Zeke followed their gaze and saw the lone figure of Clete Jameson approaching. He saw the sheriff dismount from his horse and walk across to speak to Seth and Judah.

Zeke had a sinking feeling in the pit

of his stomach as he watched Clete talking and Seth and his father listening, at first with astonishment, then anger. Clete finished his tale then stared at the ground, fingering his Stetson, as Judah Shaw raged at him.

Zeke was unable to hear what was being said but somehow knew that his plan to have McCade eliminated had gone wrong, and that Charlie Newton had failed.

This was confirmed some minutes later when his brother burst into his room with the news.

'Charlie Newton's dead,' Seth announced without preamble. 'Shot by McCade. Seems Charlie was tryin' to kill McCade, but wasn't fast enough.' His eyes had a crazed, almost excited, look in them.

'Maybe McCade riled Charlie sometime after I left him in the saloon yesterday,' Zeke said. 'Who'n hell knows!' He looked away, unable to meet his brother's eye.

'You're a piss-poor liar, Zeke!' Seth said, laughing. 'Accordin' to Clete, Charlie had fifty bucks on him. Is that why you came home early last night? Suddenly get short of money?'

'OK!' Zeke admitted. 'So I paid Charlie to kill the son-of-a-bitch! So what?'

'So you're plumb loco, like everybody says you are,' Seth said. 'An' Pa's gonna have your hide if'n he finds out what you did. Reckon he's already got his suspicions.'

'Where is Pa?' Zeke asked, suddenly looking like a trapped bear.

'He's takin' Mamie into town in the buggy,' Seth said. 'She needs a few things an' he needs to go to the bank. Best make yourself scarce for a few days before he comes back. Stay at the saloon.'

Zeke sighed. 'Yeah, OK,' he said. 'Let me know when Pa cools down.'

'You realize he's gonna guess what you did, don't you?'

'Yeah,' Zeke said, his eyes a fusion of fear and madness.

'Just get some things together an' skedaddle. I'll ride into town with you.'

Seth left the room, chuckling.

16

Three o'clock that afternoon found Jim Cranston sitting with Cody at a table in Porky Tyler's café, mulling over the events of the morning. Porky stood at their side, coffee pot in hand.

'I warned Clete,' Porky was saying. 'Tol' him Charlie was watchin' for you, Mr McCade.'

'And Clete took no notice?' Jim said.

Porky shook his head. 'Tol' me I was imaginin' things. But I knowed different.'

'Seems you were right,' Cody said.

'Zeke won't leave it like this,' Jim said.

'No, I guess he won't,' Cody said. He put his hand over his coffee mug as Porky was about to pour again. 'No more,' he said. He pushed his chair away from the table and stood up. 'Reckon I'll ride out to the Triple S an' talk to Judah Shaw. From what I saw of him last night, I don't gauge him to be a man lookin' for trouble. Maybe he can talk some sense into his hot-headed son an' avoid any further killin'.'

'No need to ride out to the Triple S,' Porky told him. 'I seen Judah Shaw drop his wife off at the mercantile then go to the bank about an hour ago. Ain't seen him come out since. Mamie Shaw went to the hotel after she left the mercantile. She'll be waitin' there until Judah collects her to go back to the ranch.'

'Then I'll pay a visit to the bank,' Cody said.

★ ★ ★

Sadie scooped up the coins on the nightstand next to her bed and pushed them into a drawer. She watched the *hombre* who'd left the money depart from her room.

She sighed and stared at the bruises on her thigh, remembering how they'd been inflicted by Seth Shaw. 'He's a mean bastard,' she muttered to herself.

'Who's a mean bastard?' Miss Lorelei asked, coming through the door that the man had left half-open.

Sadie jumped. 'Hell, Lorelei, you scared me. I was thinkin' about Seth Shaw.'

'Quit worryin' about him,' Lorelei told her. 'He ain't comin' back. He's barred.' She spoke confidently, but Sadie knew she'd be less sure about Judah Shaw's reaction to the ban she'd put on his son. 'You hear about the shootin' this mornin'?'

Sadie nodded. 'Yeah, I heard Charlie Newton got hisself killed.'

'Word is, Charlie was gunnin' for a man called McCade,' Lorelei said. 'An old army buddy of Clete Jameson.'

'What'd Charlie have against this man McCade?' Sadie asked.

'Nothin', from what I've heard. Most likely he was in the pay of Zeke Shaw, after McCade took Zeke's gun away from him an' humiliated him in front of

Miss Barrett. She wanted Zeke to leave, an' he wouldn't. So this McCade fella' kinda insisted. Real chivalrous, protectin' the lady. Anyway, Zeke started to draw his gun. McCade was too quick for him, though.'

'Zeke's dangerous, like his brother,' Sadie said. 'I hate both of them!'

'I remember when his ma died,' Lorelei said. 'Coupl'a hellions, those boys were, after that. Robbed banks, held up stages, killed anyone who got in their way. Judah closed his eyes to it, too wrapped up in his own grief to care. Not now though. He rules 'em with an iron fist these days. Even so, they're deadlier than a pair of rattlesnakes when they're roused.' She walked across to the bed and put an arm round Sadie's shoulder. 'Take it easy for the rest of the day, kid. I'll fend off anyone who comes in askin' for you.'

Sadie nodded. 'Thanks, Lorelei.'

After the older woman had left the room, Sadie eased herself from her bed and gathered up a wrap from a chair. When she'd covered her naked body, she walked across to the window and looked out.

Crossing the road was a tall man with black hair and lean, sun-bronzed features.

Is that McCade? she wondered.

She watched him make his way towards the bank and enter the building.

Some minutes later, she saw Seth and Zeke Shaw ride into town, heading towards the livery.

Sadie muttered to herself. 'Maybe this McCade fella'll kill one of them next time they try somethin'. I sure as hell hope so, 'specially if it's Seth! It'd be one less Shaw to worry about.'

17

One of two tellers looked up as Cody entered the bank. A customer — a woman — was paying in money at one of the tellers' cages. She turned in his direction. No one spoke.

Cody walked to the unoccupied cage and tipped his hat to the teller. 'Name's McCade,' he said. 'Here to see Judah Shaw.'

At that moment, Shaw stepped from an office at the back of the room. He looked ready to depart for the day but stopped short when he saw Cody. His eyes narrowed.

'You wanting to see me, McCade?' he said.

Cody nodded.

'Come on through,' Shaw said, opening a flap in the counter.

Cody followed him to the small office.

'Take a seat,' Shaw said, settling himself in a swivel chair behind a large oak desk. 'How can I help you?'

'Charlie Newton,' Cody said.

Shaw frowned, his eyebrows meeting in the middle. 'A good man,' he said. 'My foreman. Clete Jameson tells me he tried to kill you. That right?'

'Seems that way,' Cody allowed.

'It doesn't make sense,' Shaw said. 'Unless he mistook you for someone else.'

'Like who?'

'No idea,' Shaw said. 'Maybe someone he knew. Someone he perceived to be a threat. You never knew with Charlie, he always kept his cards close to his chest.'

'Some folks think he might've been in the pay of your son Zeke,' Cody said quietly.

Shaw slammed a fist down on his desk. 'Now that's a damn lie!' he said, a little too forcefully to be convincing.

The two men stared at one another in silence for several seconds. Finally,

Cody smiled and stood up.

'OK, Shaw,' he said, quietly.

At that moment, the office door opened and Cody turned to see a woman walk in.

'Mamie!' Shaw said, looking surprised. 'I thought we arranged for me to pick you up from the hotel when I'd finished here.'

Mamie Shaw looked directly at McCade and, without taking her eyes from him, said, 'I got tired of waiting, Judah.'

Shaw looked from one to the other, then said, 'This is Mr McCade, Mamie. McCade, this is my wife.'

Cody took off his hat and held out a hand. 'Glad to meet you, Mrs Shaw,' he said.

She smiled and took the proffered hand. 'You, too, Mr McCade. From what I hear, you've been — uh — causing quite a stir since you arrived in Genesis.'

'Not my intention, ma'am,' Cody replied. 'An' I'm sorry if — '

'Oh, please don't apologize,' Mamie said with an even broader smile. 'You could turn out to be just the kind of man this town needs.' She looked at her husband, a wicked gleam in her eye. 'Don't you agree, Judah?'

Shaw was silent for a good ten seconds before he said, 'We'll see.'

There was an uncomfortable silence for several moments, then Cody said, 'Guess we'll be seein' one another again, Shaw.'

'Guess we will,' Shaw agreed with a sigh.

'Afternoon, ma'am,' Cody said, and took his leave.

'Nice man,' Mamie said. 'Don't you think so, Judah?'

Shaw made no reply.

★　★　★

Zeke Shaw left his horse at Oakie Dawson's livery stable. Seth waited outside.

'You stayin' in town for a few days,

Zeke?' Oakie asked, his curiosity obvious. 'Unusual for you, ain't it?'

'Yeah,' Zeke said. 'Got a coupl'a things to attend to.'

'Your pa don't need you at the ranch?'

'If'n he did, I wouldn't be here, would I?' Zeke snapped. 'Why all the damn questions, Oakie? What's on your mind?'

'No offence, Zeke,' Oakie said quickly. 'You go right ahead. I'll take care of your horse.'

Zeke joined his brother outside. It was at that moment they both saw Cody emerge from the bank.

'That's the bastard who killed our foreman!' Zeke told Oakie, pointing at McCade and raising his voice so that the other man could not fail to hear him.

Cody paused momentarily in his stride, glanced in Zeke's direction, then walked on.

'Hey, you!' Zeke yelled after him. 'Yellow belly! Gonna try an' take my gun away again? 'Cause it'll be the last thing you do!'

'Easy, Zeke,' Seth warned his brother.

Cody kept walking. Suddenly, there was an explosion from a .45 and the dust in front of his feet skittered across his boots as the bullet hit the ground.

He stopped, turned slowly, his arms by his sides. 'Take it easy, Zeke,' he said. 'Don't do anythin' you and your pa will regret.'

'Somebody fetch the sheriff, afore there's a killin'!' Oakie yelled.

'Nobody move!' Zeke shouted.

And nobody did.

'Don't be a damn fool, Zeke,' Seth said in a low voice. 'You ain't that fast a draw. He's likely to kill you!'

'Maybe, maybe not,' Zeke said. 'Reckon he's all show. Reckon he took Charlie Newton by surprise.'

Seth sighed and shoved him aside. 'Keep your damn gun holstered an' leave the critter to me,' he said.

Seth took up the stance of a man in a stand-off. A handful of passers-by retreated to the safety of the boardwalks and stood watching. Zeke, frustrated but willing to concede his brother was faster with a gun, moved aside.

Seth looked at Cody. 'Go for your gun!' he shouted. 'Now!'

Seth wrenched his .45 from his belt — and screamed as a bullet hit him an inch above his knee.

He dropped his six-shooter, clasped his leg with both hands and stared unbelievingly as blood seeped through his pants and his fingers. Whimpering, he lifted his head up and gaped at Cody.

But Cody wasn't looking in his direction. Neither was there any tell-tale smoke coming from the barrel of Cody's Peacemaker. Instead the other man was staring silently at someone outside the bank.

Seth, sobbing with pain, turned to look.

'Pa?' he cried. 'Why . . . ?'

Judah Shaw stood outside the bank doors, his Winchester still raised and pointing in Seth's and Zeke's direction. 'To save your damn life!' he shouted. He turned to the two men nearest to him on the boardwalk. 'Help my son across to Doc Hamlin's surgery,' he said. 'Zeke, get back to the Triple S. Now!'

The men complied, supporting Seth as he half-hopped down the street, his face contorted with pain. Mamie Shaw had come out of the bank behind her husband, but she made no move to follow her stepson. Zeke hesitated for less than a minute before retrieving his horse from the livery and heading out of town at speed.

Judah walked across and picked up Seth's gun from where it had been dropped.

'Guess you need to rein in those two boys of yours, Shaw,' Cody said, holstering his weapon and walking over to join the ranch owner. 'Before they get themselves killed.'

Judah sighed. 'Listen, let me buy you a drink, McCade. As a kind of apology for my sons.'

Cody stared at him for several moments, then said. 'OK.'

The two men walked towards the Silver Buck whilst Mamie Shaw sighed and made her way back to the hotel to await her husband.

18

The two men sat at a table in the Silver Buck and regarded one another over their glasses. Cody's drink was a beer, Shaw's a whiskey.

'Tell me about Phil Temple,' Cody said.

Judah Shaw's eyes narrowed. 'Why'd you want to know about him?'

'Just satisfy my curiosity.' Cody said.

'What've you heard?' Shaw asked.

'Just that Temple vanished one night, and that he stole $2,000 from your bank,' Cody said.

'That's about it,' Judah said.

'Well now, how would he have managed that?' Cody asked. 'He have a key to the bank and the safe?'

Shaw shook his head. 'Broke in. Busted the lock on the safe.'

'And $2,000 went missing?'

'That's right.'

'Who found the safe broken into and the money missin'? One of your tellers?'

'Yes, he found it first thing when he arrived for work,' Shaw answered.

Cody stared out of the window. 'Kinda strange, don't you think?' he said, after a moment. 'From what I've heard, Temple was an honest, conscientious man doing a good job. Don't sound the kinda guy to suddenly turn bad without reason.'

Shaw shrugged. 'Who knows why a man turns bad? Anyway, the fact is, money went missing from the bank and Temple left town suddenly. Seems likely the two are connected.'

'An' Ben Paton?' Cody asked. 'Another mystery?'

Shaw stared at Cody for several seconds without speaking. Then he said, 'You sure ask a lot of questions, mister.'

Cody shrugged. 'Just curious.'

'Paton's place was burned out by Indians,' Shaw said.

'An' the men workin' for him?'

It was Shaw's turn to shrug. 'Guess they got scared and hightailed it.'

At that moment, Clete Jameson entered the saloon, glanced around the room, then made his way across to their table. He was bleary-eyed and his walk was unsteady.

'I just heard what happened, Judah,' he said. 'Seth gonna be OK?'

Judah eyed him with distaste. 'He'll live,' he said. 'I guess you slept through the shooting, Clete.'

'I was takin' a siesta, Judah, otherwise I'd've heard it,' Clete admitted, a sheepish look on his face.

'Siesta?' Shaw said. His voice hardened. 'Sure you don't mean a drunken stupor?'

Clete ran a hand across his lips. 'Gee now, that ain't fair,' he began.

'Save it, Clete,' Shaw said, dismissing him. 'Get out of my sight.'

Cody watched his old friend make as if to totter across to the bar, then change his mind and make for the batwings.

'You knew him in the war?' Shaw said.

Cody nodded. 'He was my major for a time.' He looked at Shaw. 'That's another thing that puzzles me. Seems Clete started drinking heavily and kinda went to pieces after his wife died in a stage hold-up. That was some time before Phil Temple left town. So how come the town — or, more accurately, you — made him sheriff?'

Shaw returned his gaze unwaveringly. 'Guess we made a mistake,' he said evenly.

Cody gave a rueful smile. 'Or Clete did,' he said. He drained his glass and stood up. 'Thanks for the drink, Shaw. Guess I'll be going.'

Shaw watched him leave, his expression darkening by the second. After several minutes, he got up and went to collect his wife from the hotel.

She was waiting in the lobby, hands in her lap and a bored expression on her face.

'I don't suppose you've been to Doc

Hamlin's to see how your son is faring,' her husband said, icily.

'Stepson, Judah,' Mamie said, indifferently. 'No, I haven't. But I suggest we collect him now and take him home, before he gets himself into more trouble.'

Shaw turned on his heel. Mamie smiled to herself and made no attempt to follow him. She watched him cross the street to Doc Hamlin's house.

Doc Hamlin shook his head. 'He's not here, Judah. I dressed his leg and suggested he rested up here for a while, but he hobbled out of my surgery half an hour ago with the crutch I loaned him.'

Shaw swore.

'OK, doc,' he said. 'Thanks.'

Should he go looking for his son, or head back to the Triple S and hope the stupid kid had gone home? He walked back to his wife, who was waiting in the buggy. Mamie, he decided, looked hot and tired and in no mood for a prolonged search.

'He's left the doc's,' Judah told her. 'At least I have his gun, so that should keep him out of trouble.' He tried not to think about the ease with which Zeke had acquired another .45 after McCade had taken his away. Seth would have no trouble doing the same.

19

Seth watched his father drive out of the town. He was concealed in the shadows of the boardwalk a hundred yards away. His leg throbbed painfully, but he was able to bend his knee and straighten his leg as he sat on the bench outside the barbershop, the wooden crutch at his side.

Fifteen minutes earlier, he'd seen McCade leave the saloon and walk up the street towards the Barrett rooming house. Then, minutes later, saw Judah Shaw leave the Silver Buck and go to the hotel to collect Mamie.

Seth had no intention of returning to the Triple S, not for a few days, anyway. He didn't want to face Judah's wrath or the withering looks from his step-mother. What he needed was a drink.

Or, better yet, a woman.

As if in answer to his wish, he saw

Miss Lorelei walking across the street towards the mercantile. Which meant the route to Sadie's room would be unprotected!

Seth grinned and heaved himself up from the bench, tucking the crutch under his armpit.

Sadie was sitting in her chemise, counting the dollar bills which she had removed from under a loose floorboard under her bed. It represented her entire savings — the money she kept back from Miss Lorelei after overcharging her 'clientele'. One hundred and fifteen dollars and twenty cents. Not yet sufficient to bankroll her escape from Genesis, but it was mounting up nicely.

She had just restored the money to its hiding place when the door of her room burst open. She whirled round to see Seth Shaw grinning in the doorway. His leg was bandaged under his torn jeans, and he was leaning on a crutch.

'Wh-what're you doin' here, Seth?' she said, her voice shaking. 'If Miss Lorelei — '

'Miss Lorelei ain't here,' Seth broke in, a crooked grin on his face. 'Just seen her crossin' the street.' He hobbled across to the bed and pushed Sadie back on to it. 'Now, let me think, where was we before Miss Lorelei busted in the other day?'

He clawed at the front of her chemise.

Sadie knew she had to act fast if she was to avoid more of Seth's brutality. She rolled away from him, grabbing the crutch so that he toppled sideways and crashed to the floor, cursing. Without hesitating, Sadie brought the wooden crutch down on his temple — three, four, five, six times! Then, breathing heavily, she slumped back on the bed.

Seth lay unmoving, blood streaming down his forehead.

After a moment, Sadie stooped down beside him. She listened for the sound of his breathing.

Heard nothing.

'Sweet Jesus!' Sadie whispered. 'I've killed him!'

'An' he ain't no loss to the world,' Miss Lorelei said, appearing in the doorway.

Unhurriedly, she crossed the room and helped Sadie to her feet. 'Steady now, girl.'

Sadie started to explain, but Miss Lorelei stopped her.

'Later,' she said. 'Right now we have to think about getting him outa here. Ain't no way Clete Jameson's gonna believe you was actin' in self-defence when it's one of the Shaws that's dead. Clete'll take his cue from Judah Shaw, an' Judah'll not want it spread around that his son got killed tryin' to rape a girl, even if'n that girl's a whore.'

'So wh-what we gonna do, Lorelei?'

'We're gonna keep him here until after dark — maybe until after midnight — then take him out the back way. Put him in the alley, back of the saloon. It'll be mornin' afore he's found.'

'How we gonna do that?' Sadie wanted to know. 'He ain't no light-weight.'

'We'll manage,' Lorelei said. 'Then we come back an' clean the blood off the floorboards as best we can.' She put an arm round the girl's shoulder. 'You won't be havin' any more clients today, Sadie.'

20

At eight o'clock the following morning, Clete Jameson thumped on the door of the Barrett rooming house.

Breakfast over, Owen Barrett and Cody were sitting in the living room enjoying a smoke and talking about their times in the war. Jim Cranston was in the kitchen, helping Cathy with the dishes.

Cathy broke off from her chores to answer the door.

'McCade here?' Clete demanded of her.

'Why, yes, Sheriff,' Cathy said. 'Come on in.'

Jim appeared behind her and followed them into the living room.

Cody looked up as they came in. 'You looking for me, Clete?'

'Sure am,' Clete said, his face a mixture of anger and exasperation.

'Gonna lock you up for your own safety. Damn it, McCade! I tol' you to stay outa trouble.'

Cody sighed. 'You want to tell me what this is all about, Clete?' he said.

'Seth Shaw's murder, that's what it's about!' Clete shouted.

Cathy gasped and put a hand to her mouth.

'Seth Shaw's dead?' Owen said.

'Sure is. Found dead in the alleyway behind the saloon two hours ago,' Clete said. He stared hard at Cody.

'I know nothin' about it,' Cody said. 'When was he killed?'

'Doc Hamlin reckons he's been dead at least fourteen or fifteen hours. Prob'ly killed yesterday afternoon. Beaten to death with the wooden crutch he'd been usin'.'

'I was here, yesterday afternoon,' Cody said. 'Never went out again after I left Judah Shaw at the saloon.'

'Anybody here vouch for that?' Clete asked. 'You here yesterday afternoon, Cathy?'

'Well . . . no, as it happens, I wasn't,' she admitted. 'I was at the church, with the needlepoint group. We're making kneelers for the pews.'

'You, Cranston?' Clete said.

Jim shook his head. 'I was at the newspaper office.'

'An' Owen was having his usual afternoon sleep,' Cody put in, before the older man could lie for him. 'I was here on my own, tryin' to figure out how I could help you out of the mess you seem to have got yourself into, Clete, playin' lapdog to the Shaws.'

Clete fumed, barely able to contain himself. 'Get on your feet, McCade,' he rasped. 'You're comin' with me.' He put his hand on the six-shooter at his side, as if to emphasize the point.

Cody shrugged. 'OK, Clete, I'll play it your way — for the time bein'.' He pulled himself from his chair.

'Who put you up to this?' Owen asked Clete. 'Judah Shaw?'

'Judah an' Zeke Shaw are bringin' charges against McCade here, yeah,'

Clete allowed. 'Everybody knows Seth tried to kill McCade yesterday. Ain't no surprise McCade'd want to protect himself from a surprise attack by gettin' in first.'

'You're a damn fool, Jameson!' Owen said. 'A drunken fool!'

'Enough!' Clete shouted, drawing his .45 and waving it at Cody. 'Let's get out of here, McCade.'

'Put the gun away, Clete, or I might make you use it,' Cody said. 'I'll come with you for now, until we can sort this mess out.'

'Who found Seth?' Cody asked, as he and the sheriff walked along the street.

'Barkeep at the saloon,' Clete said.

'Was Seth killed in the alleyway?'

Clete hesitated. 'Guess so,' he said.

'You're not sure?' Cody said. 'If he was beaten to death there, there'd be blood in the alleyway. Was there?'

'Some,' Clete said.

'Only some? Anyway, if the doc's right, and Seth was killed yesterday afternoon, how come nobody found him before this mornin'? He couldn't have been lying in the passageway all that time unnoticed.'

Clete looked unhappy and confused. 'Quit playin' detective,' he said.

Judah and Zeke Shaw were waiting at the sheriff's office. Both men looked ready to lynch Cody there and then. Chalky Smith stood to one side of them, looking nervous.

'I've brought him in, like you asked, Judah, but he reckons he was at the roomin' house yesterday afternoon, after leavin' you at the saloon,' Clete said.

'Anybody vouch for him?' Judah asked, his eyes fixed on Cody.

'Nope,' Clete said.

Cody stared back at the older man. 'You're makin' a mistake, Shaw,' he said calmly.

'We'll let a judge see about that!' Judah Shaw said.

'If I had my way, we'd string you up now!' Zeke snarled.

'Hold on, Zeke,' Clete put in.

'There'll be no lynchin' while I'm sheriff. Gotta let the law take its course.' He looked across at Chalky. 'You sent that wire for Judge Ford?'

Chalky nodded. 'Ten minutes ago, Clete,' he said.

'So we can expect to see him in a few days, Judah,' Clete said. 'Meantime I'll keep McCade here.'

21

'I can't believe Mr McCade had anything to do with Seth Shaw's death,' Cathy said.

'Me neither,' Jim Cranston agreed. 'But who did?'

'Could've been somebody Seth angered,' Owen said. 'We all know how hot-tempered he could be.'

They were sitting in the kitchen of the rooming house, Owen in his wheelchair.

'Zeke and Judah Shaw were pretty darn quick deciding Cody was the culprit,' Jim said, 'and charging him with Seth's murder.'

Owen nodded, thoughtfully. 'I have the feeling Judah Shaw already sees McCade as some kind of threat to his authority, even though McCade's only been in town a day or so. This is one way of getting rid of him.'

'Pretty drastic,' Jim said.

'Shaw's a ruthless man,' Owen said.

'What can we do, Pa?' Cathy said. 'Surely we've got to help Mr McCade if we can.'

'It would help if we could figure just who did kill Seth,' Jim said, standing up. 'I'll ask around, see what I can find out.'

'Be careful,' Owen told him. 'The Shaws don't take kindly to any kind of interference, which is how they'll see it.'

★ ★ ★

Sadie was scared. Every time she looked at the floorboards beside her bed and saw the faded bloodstains that she and Miss Lorelei had been unable to erase completely, her stomach heaved and she started shaking.

She had never killed anyone in her life before yesterday. And the nightmarish task of carrying Seth Shaw's body down the stairs and out to the alleyway at the back of the saloon without waking any of the other girls had haunted her dreams.

She had to get out of Genesis.

And, as luck would have it, there was a stage due in from Brynstone the next day. It would make an overnight stop, then go on to Echo Pass, fifty miles away, in the morning.

Sadie planned to be on that stage.

But first she had to tell Miss Lorelei. And she had to do it without giving away the fact that she had more than a hundred dollars that her employer knew nothing about. Because, if Miss Lorelei did learn of the money . . . well, Sadie didn't want to think about that.

So she had to do it without rousing suspicions.

Miss Lorelei was in her parlour, finishing a late breakfast. She looked up as Sadie came in. Noted the sickly pallor of Sadie's face.

'You OK, girlie?' she said. 'You ain't lookin' so good.'

'I didn't sleep too good,' Sadie replied.

'Worryin' about that son-of-a-bitch, Seth Shaw?' Miss Lorelei said. 'Then don't. I told you, the world's a better place without him. You prob'ly did us all a favour.'

Sadie picked at her fingernails and looked at her feet.

'There somethin' else?' Lorelei asked.

'I — I've decided to leave Genesis,' Sadie said. 'I'm goin' to catch the stage to Echo Pass tomorrow.'

Miss Lorelei stared at her. 'You got the fare?' she said after a moment.

'I've got a few dollars I've saved from what you pay me,' Sadie said. 'An' I thought maybe you could let me have what you owe me for this week.'

Miss Lorelei poured herself a second cup of coffee before answering. 'You sure about this, Sadie? What's in Echo Pass for you? You know anybody there?'

'A cousin,' Sadie lied.

Miss Lorelei raised her eyebrows. 'Is

128

that right? Well, OK, then. Come an' see me before you leave, an' I'll give you what I owe you.' She sighed. 'I guess I've got Seth Shaw to blame for losin' my best, most popular girl.'

22

Zeke Shaw went across to the Silver Buck after leaving the sheriff's office. Judah Shaw went to see Jed Collins to make arrangements for Seth's funeral, then went on to the bank.

Sitting at a table next to the window, over a glass of whiskey, Zeke had time to think. And scheme. He had no intention of waiting for some judge to arrive in town to preside over McCade's trial, and maybe set the critter free.

It wasn't something Zeke planned to discuss with his father. He wasn't certain how Judah would react to the suggestion. But he'd made up his mind. There wasn't going to be any trial. McCade would be a dead man before any judge set foot in Genesis.

The trouble was, however much he tried to stifle the notion, part of Zeke half-believed that McCade had been telling the truth when he'd claimed he hadn't killed Seth.

But if not McCade, then who?

And there was another thing. Just why had McCade come to Genesis? From what Zeke could make out, the stranger was no special friend of Clete Jameson, even if the two had known one another during the war. So was he just passing through? If so, it was certain the folks he'd met would have warned him that Judah owned the town and that he didn't take kindly to anyone riling him or his sons. It seemed like McCade had planned to stir up trouble with the Shaws.

But why?

* * *

Jim Cranston spent most of the morning trying to find people who had seen Seth Shaw after Doc Hamlin had patched up Seth's injured leg. As usual, when asked questions about any of the Shaws, folks clammed up. But by mid-morning, Jim had established that Seth had spent some time sitting on the bench outside the barbershop, observing events. But it was later that Josh Picard, an old-timer who had been having a shave in the barbershop the previous afternoon, gave Jim his first bit of useful information.

'Saw him makin' his way across to Miss Lorelei's,' Josh told Jim. 'Seth watched Lorelei go to the mercantile, then he hobbled across to the whorehouse. 'Bout a minute or two before Lorelei went back herself.'

'Did you see Seth go inside?' Jim asked.

'Yep,' Josh said. 'T'ain't no secret he liked that young Sadie. Reckon that's who he was headin' for.'

'Did you see him leave?'

'Nope,' Josh replied. ''Course, he might've come out when I wasn't lookin'.'

'Thanks, Josh,' Jim said. 'I think I'll pay Miss Lorelei a visit — just to ask a few questions,' he added quickly.

Josh chuckled. 'I believe you — I guess.'

It was only Jim's second visit to Miss Lorelei's establishment. The first had been a month or so after being made editor of the *Bugle*. Prior to that, he'd never had either the nerve or the money to go there.

It had not been a complete success — well, he had been a good deal younger then — and now he was 'saving himself' for Cathy Barrett.

Even so, Lorelei recognized him.

'Well, well, if it ain't young Mr Cranston!' she said with a smile. 'To what do we owe this pleasure?'

'Just some information,' Jim said quickly, his face colouring. He glanced round the parlour, in which most of the furnishings seemed to match its owner's plum-coloured hair.

'Information?' Lorelei said, her eyebrows arching.

'Yes,' Jim said. 'Seth Shaw came here yesterday afternoon.'

Lorelei licked her lips and patted her

hair before answering, 'He did? How'd you know?'

'Somebody saw him come in,' Jim told her.

'Well, then I guess he did,' she allowed. 'Can't say I saw him, but that don't mean nothin'. Why you askin' about Seth?'

'You heard he was killed?' Jim said.

'Oh, sure,' Miss Lorelei said. 'Nasty place to die, in an alleyway.'

'Yes,' Jim said. 'Listen, could I speak with one of your girls?'

'Which one?' Lorelei said.

'Her name's Sadie, I think.'

Miss Lorelei shook her head. 'Sadie ain't feelin' so good today. She's restin'.'

'Oh,' Jim said. 'Maybe later, then.'

'Actually, I don't reckon she'll be up to seein' visitors today,' Lorelei said.

The two of them eyed each other silently for almost a minute, then Jim said, 'Guess I'll be going then.'

Once out in the street, he headed back to the rooming house. Cathy was at the schoolhouse where she helped out occasionally. Owen was dozing in his wheelchair. He woke as Jim came in.

'What've you learned?' he asked the young man.

Jim gave him account of his enquiries around the town, the information he'd got from Josh Picard and his visit to Miss Lorelei's.

'What're you saying? That you believe one of Miss Lorelei's girls could've had something to do with Seth Shaw's murder?' Owen asked.

Jim nodded. 'Miss Lorelei was kinda cagey, and very protective of a girl called Sadie — a favourite of Seth's from what I've heard.'

Owen frowned, 'Well, clearly you've got to talk to this girl Sadie.'

'Agreed,' Jim said. 'Question is, how do I get past Miss Lorelei?'

'Meantime, I don't like the idea of McCade locked up in Clete Jameson's jail,' Owen said. 'He's a sitting target if Judah or Zeke Shaw decided to pre-empt any trial and put a bullet in him.'

'So let's get him out of the jail,' Cathy said from behind them.

They looked up to see her coming into the room.

'I thought you were at the school,' Owen said.

'I was,' she said. 'We finished up early.'

'And you've been eavesdropping on our conversation,' Owen said. He shook his head. 'You get more like your mother every day. I never could keep anything from her either.'

'So how do I go about helping Cody get out of jail?' Jim wanted to know.

'You don't, I do,' Cathy said.

'Wait a minute — ' Owen began.

'Listen, which of us will appear the least threatening to Clete Jameson or Chalky Smith?' she said, 'Not you, Pa, or Jim.'

'She's right, Owen,' Jim said. 'Chances are, Clete will be drinking in the Silver Buck, so it'll be Chalky Smith that Cathy will have to — er — distract.'

Owen sighed. 'I guess you have a point.' He looked at his daughter. 'But be careful, missy.'

Cathy nodded, 'I will, Pa. I'll go after dark.'

23

From his vantage point next to the window in the Silver Buck, Zeke saw Jim Cranston enter Miss Lorelei's and emerge again some minutes later. Now what, he asked himself, was that young buck doing visiting the whorehouse? He hadn't been in there long enough to avail himself of the services of any of the girls.

Then, remembering Cranston's job, it occurred to Zeke that the young newspaperman may have been following up a story. And there was only one story worth following up right now, wasn't there, and that was the murder of Seth. So what was the connection between Seth and Miss Lorelei's whorehouse?

Sadie.

Seth's favourite whore. Could Sadie have had something to do with Seth's death? Something Jim Cranston had found out about?

Zeke swallowed the last of his whiskey and headed next door.

Miss Lorelei looked surprised to see him. 'Been a while since you paid us a visit, Zeke,' she said. 'Thought you and Cathy Bassett — '

'Sadie,' Zeke cut in. 'Which room?'

Lorelei looked alarmed. 'She ain't seeing — '

'Which room?'

Lorelei swallowed. 'Top of the stairs, second room on the right,' she said, after a moment. 'Only — '

But Zeke was already taking the stairs two at a time.

Sadie was packing things into a carpetbag and she gave a little scream when Zeke burst into the room.

Zeke took in the scene, then said, 'Goin' someplace, Sadie?'

'To — to visit my cousin in Echo Pass,' Sadie said.

'Kinda sudden decision, ain't it?' He took hold of the carpetbag and upended it, tipping the contents onto the bed.

'Wh-what are you — ?' Sadie's hands flew to her mouth.

'You ain't goin' anyplace until you've answered a few questions,' Zeke said.

At that moment he noticed the dark stains on the floorboards next to the bed. He stooped down for a closer look, then glanced up at Sadie's terrified face. It told him all he needed to know.

'When'd you do it, Sadie?' he said, icily. 'Last night?'

'I — I don't know what — ' Sadie began.

He grabbed her arm. 'Miss Lorelei help you move the body into the alleyway?'

'Yes,' said a voice behind him, 'I helped her.'

Lorelei stood in the doorway, arms folded and a look of defiance on her face.

'You did, did you?' Zeke said.

'Seth had it comin', Zeke,' Lorelei said. 'It wasn't the first time he'd forced himself on Sadie, half-stranglin' her. If she hadn't hit him over the head he'd have killed her. You could call it self-defence.'

Tears began to form in Sadie's eyes and she started whimpering. 'Zeke, I swear it was an accident. I — '

'Shut up!' Zeke told her. He was trying to think. Brother or no brother, he knew what Seth had been like and, although he didn't want to believe it, what Lorelei was telling him had a ring of truth about it. Seth had never willingly taken no for an answer, especially from some cheap whore, as he would have seen Sadie. Question was, what to do about it?

Zeke took a deep breath. 'OK, listen to me, both of you,' he said. 'Seth's dead, an' there's nothin' anybody can do about that now. But Pa, Clete Jameson an' half the town reckon this man McCade murdered him. Maybe we should let them go on thinkin' that.'

Miss Lorelei glanced at the frightened Sadie, then said, 'Just what I was thinkin', Zeke. No sense muddyin' the water.' She turned to the girl. 'Finish packin' and make sure you're on that Echo Pass stage tomorrow, you hear me?'

'Yes, Lorelei,' Sadie answered, clearly hardly able to believe her luck.

'What about Jim Cranston?' Zeke asked. 'Was he askin' questions about Seth?'

'He came askin' to see Sadie,' Lorelei replied. 'Didn't say nothin' about Seth.'

'OK,' Zeke said. 'If he comes back, keep him away from Sadie.' He pointed down at the floorboards. 'An' get a rug or somethin' to cover that.'

'Sure, Zeke,' Miss Lorelei said.

24

'You've got this all wrong, Clete,' Cody said. He was stretched out on the wooden bench at the back of his cell, hands clasped behind his head.

'Shut up!' Clete told him. He was sitting at his desk, his back to the cells.

'An' you know it,' Cody continued. He could see the starlit night sky through the bars of the cell window. Several hours had passed since Clete had locked him up and, since then, the sheriff had become increasingly morose.

Chalky Smith leaned against the open door between the cells and Clete's office, chewing his fingernails and watching and listening to the exchange between the two men. He was half-enjoying the sheriff's discomfort.

'What you've got to figure out, Clete,' Cody went on, 'is who else had a reason to kill Seth Shaw.'

Chalky gave a short laugh. 'No shortage of people with a grudge against one or more of the Shaws. We could make a list, eh, Clete?'

Clete rounded on the young deputy. 'Shut your damn mouth!' he yelled. He struggled to stand up, grabbing his hat from the coat stand. 'I'm goin' out for a spell. I need some fresh air.'

'And a few drinks,' Chalky muttered under his breath, as the sheriff went out of the door. He turned to look at Cody. 'Reckon you're in one helluva fix, McCade,' he said.

'Seems to me it's Clete who's in a fix, an' has been for some time now,' Cody remarked. 'Judah Shaw pullin' his strings an' tellin' him what to do.'

'Nothin' you can do about that,' Chalky said, sitting in the sheriff's vacated chair.

'Maybe,' Cody said. 'Maybe not.'

Both men looked round as the outside door swung open and Cathy Barrett entered. She was carrying a wicker basket covered with a chequered cloth.

'I've brought Mr McCade his supper, Chalky,' she said, pushing the door closed behind her. 'I trust you've no objection.'

'No, miss,' a surprised Chalky replied, standing up. He let his eyes rest approvingly on her shapely frame. ''Specially if'n you've brought some for me, too.'

Colouring slightly, Cathy eased back the chequered cloth on the basket. 'I guess Mr McCade could spare you one of my fresh-baked bread rolls.'

Chalky grinned. 'Guess he could,' he said, and took a roll from her gloved hand.

'You'll need to open the cell door for me,' Cathy said. 'Don't worry. I just plan to hand him the basket, nothing more.'

'I'll need to check it,' Chalky said, pushing the bread roll into his mouth and holding out a hand.

Still holding the basket close to her,

she lifted a corner of the cloth. He peeked inside.

'It's just cold chicken pie,' she told him. 'Careful with the dish, it's my good china.'

'It's OK, I ain't touchin' anythin'. Just need to look.' Chalky glanced at the contents of the basket and sniffed. 'Looks good, miss,' he said, 'Not sure McCade deserves it.'

He took a set of keys from the desk drawer and selected one. Cathy watched as he unlocked the cell door with one hand and held his six-shooter with the other. He nodded at her and she handed the basket across to Cody, shielding it from Chalky's sight with her body.

'Mighty thoughtful of you, Cathy,' Cody said, his eyes widening slightly as he felt something taped to the underside of the basket.

'It was no trouble,' she said, 'I daresay Chalky will pour you some coffee to go with it.' She nodded towards a pot-bellied stove in the corner of the office. A blackened coffee pot was heating on the top. She turned and looked questioningly at the young deputy.

'Er — sure, OK,' Chalky said, relocking the cell and dropping the bunch of keys on the desk.

'Then I'll bid you goodnight, Mr McCade,' Cathy said. 'I trust this misunderstanding will be quickly put right and you'll be a free man again very soon.'

Both men watched her leave.

Chalky resumed his seat behind the desk and Cody began eating.

'You find you can't finish all of that pie, McCade, then you just pass the rest over to me,' Chalky said.

'How about that coffee?' Cody said. 'Then we'll see.'

Chalky moved across to the stove, taking the blackened coffee pot from the top and pouring the liquid into two mugs.

'Miss Bassett's sure gonna make some fella a swell little wife,' he said,

'Reckon she could take a shine to me, McCade?'

'Who knows?' Cody said, through a mouthful of pie.

He watched Chalky cross the room with two mugs of coffee. The deputy put one on the desk and started to move towards Cody's cell with the other — and stopped, eyes wide and a look of astonishment on his face as he faced the .45 that Cody was pointing at him.

'Where'n hell did you — ?' he began.

'Just put the coffee down on the desk an' pick up the keys,' Cody told him, wiping crumbs of pie from his mouth. 'An' keep your hands clear of your six-shooter.'

'Aw, jeeze!' Chalky said with a heavy sigh. 'Clete's gonna kill me!'

25

Zeke Shaw sat in the Silver Buck saloon considering his options. It would be at least three days before the out-of-town judge arrived in Genesis, but Zeke didn't plan to wait much more than twenty-four hours before he meted out his own version of justice on Cody McCade. The fact that he now knew McCade wasn't responsible for Seth's death, that one of Miss Lorelei's stupid whores had done the deed, made no difference. Zeke saw McCade as a threat. Just exactly why, he couldn't have told anybody, but he did. The man's air of confidence and cool determination unsettled Zeke, as he reckoned it did Judah.

It was as if the stranger knew something. Something that could somehow undermine the control the Shaws exercised in Genesis.

But what?

It was no good relying on Clete Jameson to prise out any information, even if he was an old army buddy of McCade's. Zeke glanced across the room to a corner table where the sheriff sat alone, nursing his usual bottle of redeye and trying to concentrate on a game of solitaire.

Needing some air, Zeke swallowed the last of his whiskey and went outside onto the boardwalk. He glanced up and down the darkened street. Pools of lamplight spilled from some of the buildings, throwing shadows.

Suddenly, he saw a figure emerge from the sheriff's office and begin walking in his direction. A moment later, he saw who it was.

'Now what was she doin' visitin' McCade?' he thought.

He stepped into the street as she approached.

'Evenin', Cathy,' he said, blocking her path.

She looked startled, putting a hand

up to her throat, but quickly composed herself. 'Hello, Zeke,' she said. 'I — I was sorry to hear about Seth.'

Zeke nodded slowly. 'Yeah,' he said.

She made as if to go past him. 'Excuse me, I — '

'You been visitin' the critter who killed him?' he demanded. ''Cause Pa an' I wouldn't take kindly to that.'

'Mr McCade is — was — one of our boarders, Zeke,' she said, her voice shaking. 'His rent's paid up until the end of the week. I just took him some supper. There's no need — '

'You're just fattenin' him up for the hangman,' Zeke told her. He gripped her arm until she winced. 'In future, leave him be. Clete'll see to all the feedin' he needs. Stay away from him, you hear?'

'Yes, all right,' she said, her voice a whisper.

He put his mouth close to her ear and whispered. 'I still mean to have you, Cathy. One day soon . . . '

He released her arm and stood aside

for her to pass, then watched her walk, white-faced, the rest of the way to the rooming house.

When she had gone inside, Zeke untied his horse from the hitching post outside the saloon and headed out of town towards the Triple S.

Half an hour later, Clete pushed open the door of his office and took in the scene with a bewildered, open-mouthed stare. Chalky Smith was tied to the sheriff's chair with his belt, his neckerchief stuffed into his mouth. Behind him was an open and glaringly empty cell.

'What'n hell — ?' Clete's face paled. 'Son-of-a-bitch!' he yelled, yanking the neckerchief from Chalky's mouth and starting to unbuckle the belt. 'What happened here?'

Chalky gulped air as he spoke. 'Miss Bassett . . . came with some supper for McCade . . . checked the basket . . . she must've taped a gun under it.'

'Jeez! Judah Shaw's gonna be mad as hell!' Clete began pacing up and down the office. 'How long's he been gone?'

'Best part of an hour,' Chalky admitted. 'He could be miles outa town by now.'

'He'd need his horse for that,' Clete said. 'Let's check with Oakie.'

Oakie Dawson was dozing on a cot at the back of the livery when Clete shook him awake.

'Wh-what — ?' Oakie rubbed his eyes and stared at the sheriff.

'McCade,' Clete said without pre-amble. 'His horse still here?'

Oakie shook his head. 'He came for it a while ago.' He frowned. 'Somethin' wrong? McCade said you'd let him go. No proof or — '

'Dammit! I did nothin' of the kind!' Clete wailed. 'He broke out after wavin' a gun at Chalky here.'

''S right,' Chalky confirmed.

'How'd he get hold of a gun?' Oakie asked.

'Don't matter how he got hold of one, he just did,' Clete said. 'What matters is where'n hell is he now?' He grabbed Chalky's arm. 'C'mon, kid.'

Out in the street, Chalky said. 'Where now? The Bassett house?'

Clete nodded. 'Guess so. Even if McCade ain't there — an' I'm guessin' he ain't — Cathy Bassett's got some explainin' to do.'

Cathy had finished telling her father and Jim about her encounter with Zeke Shaw after leaving the sheriff's office. They were sitting in the parlour of the rooming house. 'Zeke's going to connect my visit to the jail with Mr McCade's escape, isn't he?' she said.

Her father nodded. 'Which means we'll get a visit from Judah Shaw when he finds out about it,' he said.

'I still reckon Sadie knows something about Seth's killing,' Jim said. 'Guess I'll have to try to see her again tomorrow. Find a time when Miss Lorelei isn't playing guard. Where d'you reckon McCade is now?'

'He hasn't come back for his things,' Cathy said. 'They're still in his room and — '

She stopped as she heard someone banging on the front door.

'Shaw?' Jim said.

'More likely Clete Jameson,' Owen said.

'I'll go,' Jim said.

He went out of the room and re-entered some moments later with Clete and Chalky.

'Reckon you've got some explainin' to do, Cathy,' Clete said. He sat himself down in a vacant chair whilst Chalky hovered in the doorway.

Cathy said nothing, just stared defiantly.

Clete sighed, 'Come on now. The only way Cody McCade got hold of a gun was from that basket of food you brought him.' He looked accusingly at Chalky. 'Which my deputy here should've checked out more thoroughly.'

Still Cathy said nothing, just stared at him.

'Aidin' an' abettin' a criminal is a serious offence,' Clete told her.

'Have you got any proof to back up what you're accusing Miss Bassett of?' Jim asked.

'You got any other explanation for McCade gettin' hold of a six-shooter?' Clete demanded, angrily.

'I don't need one,' Jim said. 'Neither does Cathy.'

Clete looked from one to the other then heaved himself out of the chair, frustration written all over his face. 'You sure as hell ain't heard the last of this,' he said. 'When Judah Shaw learns what happened . . . ' He left the threat unfinished, then, giving them one last look of disgust, turned and left the room.

Chalky followed him.

Once outside, Clete said, 'Guess I'd better go see Judah Shaw. He's gonna have to know sometime. You go back to the office.'

'Sure, Clete,' Chalky said, sounding relieved.

26

Zeke stabled his horse and made his way across to the ranch house. There were lights on in the bunkhouse and the murmur of men's voices coming from inside as Zeke went past. As he reached the corner of the building, he felt the barrel of a gun press into his side.

'Keep walkin', Zeke,' Cody said. 'We're goin' to pay your Pa a visit together.'

Zeke took in a sharp breath, then said. 'You figure you're gonna get away with this, McCade, then you're a damn fool!'

'We'll see,' Cody said.

Walking in step, they made their way up onto the porch and in through the door of the house. Across the hall was an open door giving onto a lighted study. Judah Shaw was hunched over a large desk examining an accounts book.

'That you, Zeke?' Judah said, without turning round.

'Yeah, Pa,' Zeke replied. 'An' we've got company.'

The older man whirled round, his jaw dropping when he saw Cody holding a gun to his son's head.

'Evenin', Mr Shaw,' Cody said.

Judah recovered his composure quickly. 'Seems you're a resourceful fella, McCade, getting yourself out of jail.' He gave Cody a crooked smile. 'How'd you manage it?'

'The Bassett girl helped him, Pa,' Zeke said. 'At least, that's what I reckon. She was comin' away from the jail just afore I left town. Said she'd taken McCade some supper. Must've smuggled a gun in with it, or somethin'.'

Judah gave a mirthless laugh. 'Cathy Bassett, eh? Well, well. Even so, I don't know what you're hoping to gain by coming here, McCade. You would've been smarter to have high-tailed it out of the territory while you had the chance.'

'Had one or two things to talk over before I left,' Cody said. 'Take a seat, Zeke. But first unbuckle your gun belt an' let it drop.'

After a moment, Zeke complied, then crossed to one of two empty chairs and sat down. Cody bent down and scooped up the gun belt, then pulled the other chair towards him so that it was facing the Shaws and settled himself in it, his gun resting in his lap.

'So, what's on your mind, McCade?' Judah said.

'How's your memory, Zeke?' Cody said. 'Reckon you can remember back seven years?'

Zeke shrugged, but a look of alarm was in his eyes. 'Maybe,' he said.

'Around the time you an' Seth were robbin' stores an' holdin' up stages,' Cody said. 'Remember those days?'

Zeke tried to look bored, picking at his fingernails. He said nothing.

'You an' your brother an' a man

called Brady Stein,' Cody said. 'Remember him?'

'Never heard of him,' Zeke said.

'Strange,' Cody said. ''Cause he knew you an' Seth. Told me . . . before he died.'

★ ★ ★

Clete slid from his saddle, tied his horse to the corral fence and walked across to the Triple S ranch house. He badly needed a drink before facing Judah and Zeke Shaw but resisted the urge to take the flask of redeye from his vest pocket.

He stepped up to the porch and through the door of the ranch house, surprised to find it partly open. He went inside.

He was about to call out when he heard voices coming from across the hall. To his astonishment, he recognized one of them — Cody McCade!

Moving softly across, hand on his .45, he stopped suddenly when he realized what McCade was talking about.

★ ★ ★

A flicker of panic came and went in Zeke's eyes. He licked his lips. 'The guy must've been mistaken,' he said. 'Ain't never heard of anybody called Stein.'

'Deny it all you want, Zeke,' Cody said. 'I'm more inclined to believe the words of a dyin' man.'

'You're loco!' Zeke snarled.

'Seems the three of you robbed a dozen stores an' half a dozen stages before you an' Stein had an argument which broke up the little gang,' Cody went on. 'The argument was over the killin' of the girl, wasn't it, Zeke? The murder of Rose Jameson, Clete's wife.'

'Now wait a minute!' Judah began.

'Plain loco,' Zeke repeated.

'It was you who shot her, not Seth,' Cody went on. 'She recognized you, in spite of your masked face, didn't she? Put two an' two together an' figured

161

Seth was another of the gang. An' she was right.'

'This is crazy,' Zeke said.

On hearing his dead wife's name, Clete froze, yards from the open study door but out of sight of the study's occupants. His thoughts whirled as the conversation went on, but gradually, one searing fact emerged like a locomotive bursting out of a black tunnel.

Zeke Shaw had killed Rose!

A knot of hatred formed in Clete's gut as he continued to listen. Anger burned in his chest until he found it difficult to breathe.

27

'Even assuming what you say is true,' Judah Shaw was saying calmly, 'and I'm not saying it is, what's your part in this, McCade? Something to do with Clete being an old army buddy?'

'Not exactly,' Cody said.

'Then what?' Zeke demanded suddenly.

Cody took a deep breath, letting it out slowly before beginning to speak. 'I knew Rose Jameson,' he said, 'although she was Rose Segley then. I worked on her father's spread — as a ranch hand. My folks were dead by this time an' Rose's pa and ma were the nearest thing I had to a family. This was before the war. Lost track of Rose an' her folks when the conflict started an' I joined up.'

'Let me guess,' Judah said. 'You were in love with this Rose girl.'

Cody nodded slowly. 'Yeah, I loved Rose. Never told her, not exactly, although I reckoned she had an inklin' as to how I felt. Anyways, three years into the war I served under a Major Clete Jameson. Discovered that he had married a girl he'd met at some Union fund-raisin' dance his family had organized. Well-to-do folks, the Jamesons, it seemed. Clete was the youngest of three sons. The other two were killed the first year of the war an' the dance was sorta in their memory.'

'And the girl he'd married was Rose Segley,' Judah said. He glanced at his son — who looked like a cornered prairie wolf, exuding pure venom.

Cody nodded. 'Yeah, it was Rose. I never told Jameson I knew her, not after I discovered the sorta man he was — rich, spoilt. And yellow!'

'Yellow?' Judah raised his eyebrows. 'You mean, a coward?'

'Figures,' Zeke said, softly.

'Clever at avoidin' most of the fightin',' Cody said. 'Not one to lead his men — includin' me — into an attack. Always managed to be part of the rearguard. The retreatin' rearguard, mostly. An' sent men to their deaths through bad judgement.' Cody sighed. 'Good men, too. Anyway, about a year before the end of the war, Jameson got caught embezzlin' army funds. He was reduced to the ranks after a spell in an army prison — then he disappeared. Never saw out the war, as far as I know. Never went back to his family. He an' his young wife — Rose — came west, an' disappeared.'

'They came here,' Judah said. 'I gave him a job and a place to live. But how did you track him down to Genesis?' He was clearly interested in Cody's tale, ignoring his son's discomfort.

'I heard about this Genesis sheriff called Jameson whose wife had been killed in a stage hold-up,' Cody said. 'Heard about it from another lawman. Guessed it was Clete, an' that it was Rose who'd been killed.' He paused, anguish clear on his face. 'Anyway, I

165

made it my business to learn a bit more. Started askin' around. Got the word from a bunch of no-goods that a gunman called Brady Stein was probably one of the gang who held up the stage. Spent the next year trackin' him down.'

'And killing him?' Judah said.

'Didn't need to kill him,' Cody said. 'He was dyin' anyway. Cancer. Seemed ready to get a few things off his chest, though, before he left this earth. Admitted he was one of the stage hold-up gang after I put it to him.' He looked at Zeke. 'An' told me the names of the other two — the Shaw brothers. That was a month ago. Figured it was time for me to pay a visit to Genesis an' look up my old major.'

'An' ran into a whole heap o' trouble,' Zeke said, sneering. 'Guess you didn't reckon on that, McCade.'

'You're right, he didn't,' Clete said, coming into the room, holding his .45, but pointing it at nobody in particular.

'Clete, it's good to see you!' Judah

said, thinking quickly. His right hand moved under his desk. 'And good to see you tracked down your jailbird. Smart thinking, guessing he'd come here.'

'My jailbird's got a big mouth!' Clete said, looking straight at Cody.

'But an honest one, Clete,' Cody said. 'I lost good friends due to your bad judgement. An' I ain't lyin' when I say you were always behind your troops rather than in front of them whenever the fightin' started.'

''Cause I was a whole lot smarter than you an' your like!' Clete said. 'Think I wanted to die for some damn so-called 'cause'? Then think again, mister! My two fool brothers got themselves killed an' I wasn't plannin' to follow them.'

'That why Rose was leavin' you?' Cody asked. ''Cause she realized you were yellow?'

'Shut up!' Clete snapped. 'Rose an' me had our . . . differences, sure. But I reckon she'd would've seen sense an' come back.' He turned and looked at

Zeke, levelling his gun so that it pointed directly at the other man. 'If'n she'd been given a chance. Reckon I'll give you the same chance as you gave her.'

'Now hold on, Clete!' Zeke began, his face registering sheer panic. 'I ain't — '

The shot came from Judah Shaw's .45, pulled from a clip under his desk. A red starburst exploded on Clete's chest, knocking him backwards, a look of astonishment on his face.

If Cody's attention had been momentarily distracted by Clete, he was fast enough to follow Judah's shot with one of his own. The bullet from his Peacemaker penetrated Judah Shaw's throat before exiting out of the back of his head.

Gunsmoke hung in the air as Cody gave a long sigh and got out of his chair, turning his attention to Zeke. The latter was staring open-mouthed at the dead body of his father, unable to believe what he was seeing. To him, the great man had seemed indestructible.

'I guess it's safe to come in now, Mr McCade,' came a voice from the doorway.

Cody turned to see Mamie Shaw standing there as the sound of running footsteps came from the bunkhouse outside. Mamie looked steadily at the dead bodies of Sheriff Jameson and her husband.

'Sorry, Mrs Shaw,' Cody said. 'But I guess it was always going to end this way.'

She nodded. 'I guess it was.'

28

Figures were crossing the hall and appearing behind her. They came to a halt, shock and confusion in their expressions as they took in the scene.

Bud Whitefoot, a tall, bearded man, who had assumed the role of ranch foreman since the demise of Charlie Newton, was first to speak.

'What'n blazes is goin' on here, Miz Shaw?' he said.

'If what I overheard as I came down the stairs is true,' Mamie Shaw said after a moment, 'it would seem some kind of justice has just been done.' She looked at Cody. 'Wouldn't you say, Mr McCade?'

'Reckon so,' Cody replied.

'Don't listen to him, Bud!' Zeke yelled. 'McCade just shot the sheriff an' murdered my father! An' don't listen to her. She hated Pa, an' was plannin' to

walk out on him first chance she got.'
He looked at Mamie, challenging her
to deny it. 'Think me an' Pa didn't
know what you were plannin'? Well,
we did!'

Bud's confusion was written across
his face, as it was on the faces of the
two men with him. Used to taking
orders from Judah, rather than either
of his frankly half-crazy sons, they
were unsure what to do. In the end, it
was Bud who took the decision and
acted. Whipping out his six-shooter
from its holster, he grabbed Mamie
and held the gun to her head. She
screamed and tried to break free, but
without success.

'Drop your weapon, McCade,' Bud
said.

Cody looked from Bud to Zeke,
then back at Bud. 'You're makin' a
mistake, Bud,' he said. 'Zeke Shaw
has the law to answer to, for killin'
Rose Jameson, amongst others.' He
put the fingers of his free hand into
his vest pocket and drew something

171

out. It glinted in the lamplight. 'Which is the reason I came to Genesis.'

'What is it, Bud?' one of the other two men said, trying to look over Bud's shoulder.

Bud stared. 'Looks like a US Marshal's badge,' he said. 'You — you the law, McCade?'

'I'm the most law you've got around here, now Clete Jameson's dead,' Cody told him. 'Not sure Chalky Smith is up to the job, are you? Now set Mrs Shaw free an' holster your .45.'

During this exchange, Zeke had sidled towards his father's desk. Now, moving quickly, he scooped up his father's gun from the top and dropped behind the desk for cover.

As he let off a shot, Cody dived behind the leather armchair he'd been sitting in and returned fire. But not before Zeke's bullet had sunk into his shoulder. His own shot ploughed harmlessly into the wood panelling around the walls of the room.

'This ain't no time to switch sides, Bud!' Zeke yelled. 'Nor you and Hal, Sid, neither of you. Do somethin'!'

The three ranch hands were hesitating.

'Don't fancy takin' on no US marshal, Bud,' one of the three said. 'How about you, Sid?'

'Nope, not me,' Sid answered.

And the two of them backed away.

Bud was still wavering but, in the end, released Mamie Shaw by pushing her into the room and following the other two.

Mamie stumbled forward at the same moment Zeke fired a shot at the retreating Bud. The bullet creased her arm, spinning her round. She shrieked and fell against a glass cabinet containing a collection of antique pistols. The glass shattered under the impact and the cabinet started to topple sideways. It fell in the direction of the chair Cody was crouching behind and he was forced to roll away.

Seeing this, Zeke took the opportunity to yank open the centre desk drawer, snatch a bunch of keys from it, then run towards the doorway, firing covering shots over his shoulder, all of which joined the others in the wood panelling, missing Cody by a yard.

By the time Cody had picked himself up, nursing his shoulder, and had gone to attend to the injured Mamie, Zeke was out of the house and running towards his horse.

Outside, the three ranch hands watched him from the shadows at the side of the bunkhouse, not attempting to stop him. Seconds later, Zeke was riding away from the Triple S as if the devil himself was on his tail.

'The bank!' Zeke muttered to himself. 'Gotta get to the bank.'

Some minutes later, a shout came from the house. 'Hey! Mrs Shaw needs help!' Cody was standing in the doorway, clutching his injured shoulder and peering into the darkness. 'Where'n hell are you?'

Startled into life, Bud ran towards the house.

'Get the buggy, Sid,' he shouted over his shoulder. 'Looks like I'm goin' into town.'

29

Zeke finished stuffing banknotes into his saddle-bags and took a last look around his father's office — an office the old man wouldn't be needing any more.

Zeke's head was in a spin.

McCade, a damn US Marshal!

Who the hell could have guessed that? One thing was certain, Zeke wasn't planning to hang around Genesis now the truth about Rose Jameson and the stage hold-up was out. He knew for sure that Bud and the other two ranch hands would spread the story around the town faster than a prairie fire. No, it was time to get out and make a fresh start someplace else. And, with best part of three thousand dollars in his saddle-bag, there was nothing to stop him.

He had no regrets about leaving the

Triple S. Never had enjoyed the work of cattle breeding or horse rearing. Only did it to please his pa. Well, now he could please himself. And he damn well would!

He turned off the lamp and left through the back door. His horse was out of sight in the alleyway at the rear of the building.

* * *

'Time to go,' Zeke muttered to his mount. 'But there's one other person I plan takin' with me. An' this time I ain't taking no for an answer.'

Chalky Smith was dozing on the cot in one of the two open cells at the back of the sheriff's office. He had planned to stay awake until Clete returned from the Triple S but tiredness had overtaken him.

He woke suddenly when the office door swung open and a voice yelled, 'Hey, Chalky, where's the sheriff?' It was Oakie Dawson, his nightshirt

177

stuffed into his pants. 'Somebody's been robbin' the bank!'

'Wh-what?' Chalky rolled off the cot and staggered to his feet.

'There was a lamp on in the bank,' Oakie told him. 'A minute ago, somebody came out through the back door.'

'Probably Mr Shaw,' Chalky said, nervously. He had no desire to go exposing himself to some crazy bank robber.

'Weren't Shaw,' Oakie said. 'I saw the back of a fella come from round the side of the buildin', then, minutes later, the lamps goin' on. 'Tweren't Judah Shaw.'

'What'n hell you doin' out of bed anyways?' Chalky grumbled.

'Gotta sick horse needed my attention,' Oakie told him. 'Was goin' back to bed when I looked up the street an' saw the light. Fella was inside best part of ten minutes now. You goin' to wake the sheriff?'

'He ain't here,' Chalky told him.

'Jeeze, you mean it's you whose gonna have to go after this son-of-a-bitch? Jeeze!' Oakie shook his head in despair.

It was at that moment they heard the sound of horses out in the street.

'Now what?' Chalky groaned, praying it was the sheriff come to his rescue.

The two men went outside, in time to see a buggy stop outside Doc Hamlin's house and a man help a woman from the back before going to hammer on the doc's door.

A fourth man, sitting half-slumped over his horse, watched them for a moment before heading up the street towards the sheriff's office.

'Ain't that McCade comin'?' Oakie said.

'Yeah, it is,' Chalky said. 'Oh, hell!'

He'd left it too late to retreat into the office and collect his gunbelt, which was lying beside the cot he'd been napping in. Before he could move, Cody was alongside the two men.

'Evenin', Chalky,' Cody said. 'I've got

179

some news before I go an' get Doc Hamlin to do somethin' about this bullet in my shoulder. What d'you want first, the good or the bad?'

Chalky didn't answer. Both he and Oakie were staring open-mouthed at the silver badge pinned to Cody's vest.

★ ★ ★

Cathy woke to the noise of someone breaking in the back door of the house. Moments later, there was the sound of feet running up the stairs.

She got out of bed and pulled on a robe, her heart pounding. She could hear doors being banged open and the startled shouts of her father and Jim Cranston. Then her own bedroom door flew open and she was confronted by the sight of Zeke Shaw holding the nightshirt-clad Jim Cranston around the shoulders and pressing a gun to his head. Two bulging saddle-bags were slung across Zeke's shoulders.

A leer spread across Zeke's face as he

looked her up and down. 'You'd best get some clothes on, Cathy,' he told her. 'You an' me are gettin' out of this town.'

'You're crazy, Zeke,' Jim said. 'You'll never get away with this.'

'Shut your damn mouth!' Zeke rasped. He waved the gun at Cathy. 'Get movin', girl, unless you want to see this newspaper hack get a bullet through his head. An' don't mind us. It ain't no time to get coy.'

'Wh-where's Pa?' she said.

'Sleepin' like a baby,' Zeke said. He grinned. 'I gave him a helpin' hand with the butt of my gun.'

Cathy put a hand to her mouth and gave a small cry. 'Oh! Why did you have to — ?'

'Shut up, an' dress!' Zeke shouted. 'We ain't got much time.'

Hands shaking, Cathy began to remove her robe.

30

After Cody had narrated his story of the happenings at the Triple S, Oakie repeated his suspicions about a bank robber. Cody listened, trying to ignore the pain in his shoulder but aware of a growing light-headedness caused by the loss of blood.

'It weren't Judah Shaw,' Oakie said. 'I'm pretty sure of that. Could've been Zeke though, after what you've just told us.'

Cody nodded. 'Reckon it was. Gettin' himself a stake before hightailin' it. Well, I gotta get this shoulder fixed. Guess it'll be mornin' before I can pick up his trail an' go after him.' He looked at Chalky. 'Wouldn't hurt if you got a posse together at first light.'

Chalky, still stunned by the news about Clete Jameson, nodded silently. He was only too happy to waive the decision-making and take orders from a US Marshal.

'Guess I'll get along to the doc's,' Cody said. 'Nothin' more I can do tonight. Zeke'll be long gone by now.'

'I — I ain't so sure,' Oakie said. He pointed along the street. 'Ain't that a light in an upstairs room in the Bassett place? You don't reckon Zeke's plannin' on takin' a certain person with him, do you?'

Cody swore. 'Hell, why didn't I think of that! Get your gun, Chalky!' he snapped. 'Oakie, go rouse a few folk from their beds. We're gonna need help.'

Retaining a certain amount of modesty, Cathy had put on a pair of jeans before turning away, taking off her nightdress and putting on her chemise and shirt. Now she was pulling on a pair of boots.

Jim Cranston was standing next to the window, hands in the air and watching Zeke, who was still in the doorway, gun pointing towards the young editor of the *Bugle* but eyeing Cathy.

'Hurry it up!' Zeke told her.

'I need to see if Pa's all right,' she said. 'Please Zeke, I can't — '

'No time!' Zeke growled. 'We gotta get away before that McCade fella decides to come back to his bed. Reckon he'll have to pay a visit to Doc Hamlin first though, that's assumin' he made it into town.'

'I think he did,' Jim said, the relief in his voice clear. He had eased back one of the curtains and was looking out into the street. 'He's collected a few other folk, too. Give yourself up, Zeke. You and Cathy aren't going anywhere.'

Zeke moved swiftly to the window and peered out. He could see shadows moving around the house in the semi-darkness and the tall figure of McCade directing them.

Cursing, he pushed Jim across the room to join Cathy. 'Change of plan,' he said, eyes wild with a mixture of fear and excitement. 'You, Cranston, are goin' out an' givin' McCade a message. You're gonna tell him to give me an' Cathy safe passage out of Genesis or I'm gonna put a bullet in her head. Got it?'

Jim licked his dry lips, heard himself croak the words, 'Sure, Zeke,' and tried to think.

'Go!' Zeke yelled.

Jim scrambled down the stairs and out through the front door of the house, hands in the air in case anyone outside got trigger-happy. 'It's me! Cranston!' he shouted.

'Over here!' came a reply.

Jim recognized Cody McCade's voice coming from across the street and he made his way towards it. Gradually, Cody's figure emerged from the shadows.

'He's got Cathy,' Jim told him, once they were side by side. He saw Chalky Smith standing a few feet away from Cody, holding a Winchester and looking scared. 'He says you've got to let him leave town with her, or he'll kill her. I think he means it.' He saw Cody's blood-stained shirt and the other man's grey-white complexion. 'You OK?'

'He needs a doctor,' Oakie said, coming from somewhere in the shadows and lining himself up alongside the other two. Then, addressing Cody, he added, 'Got two men coverin' the back of the house, like you said.'

'OK,' Cody replied, weakly. He could feel the light-headedness sweeping over him again.

'Somebody go get the doc!' Oakie shouted into the darkness.

Seconds later, a voice said, 'No need, I'm here.' And Doc Hamlin materialized out of the darkness with his black bag. 'But I need some light. Come on, McCade. The church is nearer than my house, we'll go there.'

'Can't,' Cody said, his voice a whisper. 'Gotta get Miss Bassett away from Zeke before . . . ' His words trailed off and, without warning, he collapsed to the ground.

'Oakie, give me a hand,' Doc said.

And the two of them half-dragged Cody along the street to the church.

But not before Jim had picked up the six-shooter Cody had dropped.

'Jeeze, what're we gonna do now?' Chalky wanted to know.

Before Jim could answer, a shout came from the darkened open doorway of the rooming house.

'One of you go get a horse for Cathy!' Zeke yelled. 'Bring it to the gate alongside mine. An' do it fast.'

'OK,' Jim shouted back. 'I'm going.' And he broke into run towards the livery. As he got near, he saw Oakie coming from the church.

'Doc says he can manage alone,' Oakie told Jim. 'Where're you goin'?'

'Zeke wants a horse for Cathy,' Jim said.

'I'll get it,' Oakie said. 'You go back — '

'No, wait!' Jim said. 'I'm coming with you. I've got an idea.'

Zeke's patience was running ragged. Standing in the doorway holding on to

Cathy's arm and with the weight of the two saddle-bags pressing down on his shoulders, he tried to see what was happening outside. Where was that damn horse? More important, where was McCade? It was the US Marshal he feared most. The man should've bled to death just getting into town, curse his luck!

Zeke saw the darkened shape of Oakie leading a horse at an angle across the street.

'Jus' hold on, Zeke!' Oakie yelled. 'Don't do anythin' hasty! I'm bringin' you the horse!'

'Stand it next to mine by the gate!' Zeke shouted. 'Then move away.'

'Sure, Zeke,' Oakie said. 'Jus' take it easy.'

He led the horse up to the gate of the rooming house and left it, reins dangling, next to Zeke's sorrel. Then he hurried back towards the safety of the other side of the street.

Zeke waited until Oakie was out of sight then, positioning himself directly behind Cathy, pushed her gently forward, his gun pressing against her back.

'Walk real slow,' he told her.

He could feel her shaking, her breath coming in short terrified gasps. But even in the danger of that moment, Zeke could not help but feel a lustful flush of excitement surge through his body, rendered by the complete control he had over her.

'Get on the horse, but take it slow,' he told her, as they approached the two animals.

Zeke's horse was nearest but he did not attempt to mount until Cathy was pulling herself up into the saddle. Then, moving rapidly, he got aboard the sorrel — only to hear the SLAP! of a hand on the rump of the other horse before it leapt several yards away, Cathy clinging to its reins and trying to steady it.

A bewildered Zeke had just enough time to register the fact that someone had been concealed behind the other animal before two bullets hit him in the chest, knocking him off his mount.

Seconds before he died, Zeke saw the fearful face of Jim Cranston looking down at him, a smoking Peacemaker in his right hand. Zeke tried to speak, but no words would come from his mouth, only a trickle of blood.

And then . . . darkness.

★ ★ ★

Cody came round and found himself lying on a bed and staring up at a strange ceiling. Aware of the dull pain in his shoulder, he twisted round and saw that it was neatly bandaged.

Doc Hamlin was sitting in a chair beside the bed. 'Gave you some laudanum to deaden the pain after I took the bullet out,' he told Cody. 'You lost a lot of blood, but you'll be OK.'

'Cathy!' Cody began, alarm in his eyes. He tried to sit up.

'Take it easy,' Doc Hamlin said, putting a restraining hand on his arm. 'Cathy's fine.'

'And Zeke Shaw?'

'Dead,' the doc said.

Cody breathed easier. 'How?' he asked.

'Jim Cranston killed him.' Doc Hamlin told him. He gave a short laugh. 'According to Oakie Dawson, Cranston turned himself into one of those heroes he writes about in those dime novels of his.'

Cody grinned. 'He did?'

Doc Hamlin nodded. 'Seems he adopted a tactic he'd written about a few times.'

'Tactic? What tactic?' Cody asked.

'He used a horse as cover to get close to Zeke, then shot the varmint twice,' the doc said.

'Smart,' Cody said.

'It was,' the doc agreed. 'Reckon Cathy Bassett thought so, too. He's her hero!'

31

Sadie handed her bag to the stagecoach driver and turned to Miss Lorelei. The two women hugged one another.

'You sure you still want to go?' Lorelei asked. 'Nobody's askin' questions about Seth's death after what happened to Judah and Zeke Shaw last night. Folks are lookin' upon it same as they would if somebody'd killed a rabid coyote. Which, near as dammit, Seth was.'

'Yeah, I'm still goin',' Sadie said. 'Too many bad memories in this town. I need a fresh start.'

She looked over Lorelei's shoulder as Jim Cranston emerged from the saloon.

Lorelei turned to face him.

'Now don't you go botherin' Sadie with any damn-fool questions, newspaperman,' she said.

Jim gave Sadie a knowing look, then

smiled. 'Hadn't planned to,' he said. 'I've got more than enough news to fill the *Bugle* this week, after everything that's been happening. In fact, enough to start a new storybook, too.'

'An' a clear run for Miss Bassett's affections now Zeke Shaw's no longer around to pester her.' Lorelei chuckled, seeing Jim's face redden. 'Aw, don't look so bashful! Everybody in town knows how you feel about her, 'ceptin' maybe the girl herself. An' ain't it about time you did somethin' about that?'

'I aim to,' Jim said. 'Same as I aim to make the *Bugle* a proper newspaper now it's no longer a mouthpiece for Judah Shaw.'

They looked up to see a buggy making a dust cloud as it sped down the street. It pulled up just short of the stage and Bud Whitefoot jumped down from the driver's seat. He began unloading bags from the rear of the vehicle.

At the same time, Mamie Shaw

stepped down from her seat at the front. Her arm was bandaged and she looked a little pale, but otherwise her demeanour was one of someone who'd had all her wishes come true at the same time.

'You leaving town, too, Mrs Shaw?' Jim asked her. He looked interested but not surprised.

'That's correct, Mr Cranston,' she said. 'I'm taking the stage to Echo Pass where I'll catch a train east.' She looked up and down the street. 'I doubt I'll return, but you never know.' She turned to Bud, who had just finished handing her bags to the stage driver. 'My lawyer will be in touch when we have a buyer for the Triple S and the bank, Bud. Meantime, you and the boys keep things ticking over at the ranch and Henry Rees will look after affairs at the bank.'

'OK, ma'am,' Bud said.

She turned to Sadie. 'Are we to be travelling together?'

'Y-yes, ma'am,' Sadie replied, embarrassed.

Miss Lorelei chuckled. 'You don't have to worry about Sadie, Mrs Shaw,' she said. 'Real . . . discreet, Sadie is. Never talks about her — uh — clients. Or mine,' she added meaningfully.

Mamie Shaw seemed about to reply, then laughed and stepped aboard the stage. Sadie, still nervous, followed her before another passenger — a drummer clutching his sample case — climbed in after them.

Miss Lorelei and Jim waited on the boardwalk until the stage disappeared from view and Bud Whitehead had made his way into the saloon. They were about to go their separate ways when both noticed a rider coming from the livery.

It was Cody McCade.

'You leaving town, too, Cody?' Jim said as he drew alongside them.

Cody halted his horse. His right arm was in a sling. 'Reckon so,' he said. 'Nothin' to keep me here now. Except for retrievin' my gun which you made such good use of, Jim.' He held out a hand.

'Oh, sure.' Jim pulled the Peacemaker from his belt. He seemed sorry to part with it. 'Just getting used to the feel of it,' he said with a grin. 'Might get myself another. What're you planning to do now, Cody?'

Cody's eyes narrowed with a glint of humour. 'Gotta give a report about all this to someone.'

'Report?' Jim said. 'Which someone?'

'Someone you might be seein' here again soon,' Cody said. He grinned.

'Who?'

'Phil Temple.'

'Temple?' Both Jim and Lorelei said the name together.

'That's the man,' Cody said.

'He ain't dead?' Lorelei said.

'Nope,' Cody told them. 'He's alive an' kickin' in Echo Pass.'

'We — everybody — thought the Shaw brothers killed him,' Jim said.

'So did the Shaw brothers,' Cody

said. 'They took him out of town at gunpoint in the night. Took him to a cave out in the hills, twenty miles north of town. Shot him, then piled rocks across the entrance of the cave. Figured it'd make a secure tomb for a dead man. But, just like the stage driver, they didn't take the trouble to check properly. Phil wasn't dead, just injured.

'Then he got lucky. An old prospector who had a cabin a coupl'a miles away was passin' an' noticed that the cave entrance had been covered over. Decided to see what it was someone was hidin' — an' found Temple. The old-timer took Temple back to his cabin, nursed him, dressed his wounds, fed an' watered him for nigh on a month. Then Phil borrowed one of the old man's mules to get him to Echo Pass, where he's been livin' ever since. Fact, he's kinda comfortable there, even got himself a girl, so maybe he won't be comin' back to Genesis.'

'We could sure use him,' Lorelei said. 'Now that Clete Jameson's dead.

Chalky ain't up to the job of sheriff.'

'I'll tell him that when I see him,' Cody said. 'Might be enough to persuade him.'

'How did you come to meet up with him?' Jim asked.

'Met him in Echo Pass after I'd finished another job,' Cody said. 'We got talkin' an' he told me about the stage hold-up an' the woman who was killed. A woman I realized I'd known — and loved.'

'Loved?' Jim said. 'Rose Jameson?'

Cody nodded. 'It's a long story. Maybe I'll tell it to you if I decide to some back here anytime.'

'Hold on, Cody,' Jim said. 'You said you met Phil Temple after you'd finished another job. What sort of job?'

'Trackin' down a bunch of bank robbers,' Cody said.

Jim frowned. 'Are you some kind of lawman?'

'Oh, I guess you didn't notice it in the darkness last night,' Cody said, a twinkle in his eye. He took the US

Marshal's silver star from his vest pocket and proceeded to pin it to his vest. 'Yeah, I'm a kinda lawman. So long.'

Before Jim or Lorelei could say anything more, he tipped his hat and rode away.

'Well, I'll be damned!' Miss Lorelei said at last.

Jim laughed. 'Yeah, Lorelei. I reckon you will.'

THE END

We do hope that you have enjoyed reading this large print book.

Did you know that all of our titles are available for purchase?

We publish a wide range of high quality large print books including:
Romances, Mysteries, Classics
General Fiction
Non Fiction and Westerns

Special interest titles available in large print are:
The Little Oxford Dictionary
Music Book, Song Book
Hymn Book, Service Book

Also available from us courtesy of Oxford University Press:
Young Readers' Dictionary
(large print edition)
Young Readers' Thesaurus
(large print edition)

For further information or a free brochure, please contact us at:
Ulverscroft Large Print Books Ltd.,
The Green, Bradgate Road, Anstey,
Leicester, LE7 7FU, England.
Tel: (00 44) **0116 236 4325**
Fax: (00 44) **0116 234 0205**

Other titles in the
Linford Western Library:

A NECKTIE FOR GIFFORD

Ethan Flagg

The bounty hunter known as 'Montero' learns that his brother is to be hanged for murder in the New Mexico town of Alamagordo. A single clue left by the dead man — the two letters 'MA' — ensures that a guilty verdict is inevitable. The two brothers had parted some years before under hostile circumstances, but Montero is convinced that Mace Gifford would never shoot a man in the back. He plans an ingenious escape, but saving his bother's neck is only the beginning — he has to find the real killer . . .

THE PHANTOM RIDER

Walt Keene

A mysterious killer is riding into each town on the plains, hell-bent on dispatching as many men, woman and children as he can. In the blood of his victims is scrawled the same message: 'The Phantom'. As the ruthless horseman travels further south, he is unaware that he is soon to face three men who could be the ones to stop his unholy carnage. For Tom Dix, Dan Shaw and the legendary Wild Bill Hickok are waiting . . .